Quest for the Pillars of Wealth

A Children's Guide to Growing Rich

Quest for the Pillars of Wealth

A Children's Guide to Growing Rich

J. J. Pritchard

LANTERN PRESS
Bainbridge Island, Washington

Lantern Press
PO Box 10771
Bainbridge Island, Washington 98110
206-344-3716

ISBN 0-9703433-0-2

Library of Congress Catalog Card Number: 00-191709

To the *real* Gennie and Jeff

൬ ൬ ൬

Contents

A Visitor from the Past 1

The Chamber of Pillars 9

THE FIRST PILLAR

The Barrier of Stone 15

Caltor the Colossus 24

Trapped in Time 29

False Hopes 34

Mortinas the Elder 40

The Puzzling Enduro 47

The Rope Wheels 57

The Strength of Ten Men 68

Racing the Sun 74

Second Chance 81

The First Pillar Is Revealed 85

THE SECOND PILLAR

Ancient Rome 93

The Secret to Augustus's Wealth 99

The Spider's Web 105

Preparing for the Feast 109

The Trap Is Sprung 115

☙ Contents ❧

Dovenia's Wrath 119

Augustus's Promotion 125

The Passageway 129

The Money Lenders 134

Indentured Servitude 141

The Dark One 145

The Wisdom of Saving 152

Gennie's Fond Farewell 156

THE THIRD PILLAR

The Shire of Worstecher 160

The Contest of Wisdom 166

Shrillmora's Silver Coins 173

Treasure in the Woods 179

The Final Counting 189

Waldor's Miracle 198

Homeward Bound 205

CHAPTER 1

A Visitor from the Past

Jeff Douglas pulled his knees close to his chest as he perched on the upstairs landing, listening to his parents arguing below.

Even with his hands covering his ears, he couldn't dodge the bitter words echoing up the stairway, hurled in anger like weapons. All the arguing, all the bitterness, all the simmering anger—it was always about the same thing—money!

Jeff didn't know much about money, or why it was such an explosive topic for his parents. He just knew that when they fought about money he always got a tight knot in his eleven-year-old stomach, an uncomfortable feeling that kept him up all night.

It had been a while since he'd eavesdropped on a biggie like this one. Lately, there had been fewer arguments. It was as if his parents had simply lost the energy to argue. They went about their routines in icy silence. He wasn't sure which he preferred—the yelling, or the deafening roar of a silent house.

Jeff's gray sweatpants were frayed and spattered with paint and glue from the models he liked to build. Although he was only in the fifth grade, his white high-tops were as big as his father's. Usually Jeff wore a wide, ready smile on his round face, which made his hazel, impish eyes shine. But there was no smile tonight. Tonight, his eyes were red with worry.

Jeff's only sibling, his older sister, Gennie, quietly opened her bedroom door and crept to Jeff's side. Unusually tenacious for a thirteen-year-old seventh grader, Gennie took on everything— school, chores, hobbies—with a 100 percent commitment. She simply didn't believe in moderation.

Tonight she had changed out of her nightgown into a pair of jeans, a long-sleeve white shirt, a denim jacket, and a pair of red Keds canvas sneakers. Her blue-gray eyes were also red and puffy.

"They're fighting again," Jeff whispered, as Gennie plopped down next to him.

"I know," Gennie said softly. "How could you not hear it?"

"What time is it?" Jeff asked tiredly.

"Two in the morning," she replied.

"Great!" Jeff said sarcastically. "Why are you dressed?"

"The same reason you're sitting on the stairs. I can't sleep with this going on. Let's sneak outside," Gennie suggested.

"I'm all for that!" Jeff said.

The two slipped quietly down the stairs and out the front door, closing the door on all those angry words, but taking their worry with them into the cold night.

Gennie and Jeff sat on the front-porch steps. They could see their breath in the cold night air. The moon was unusually bright overhead, bathing the neighborhood in a silvery blue light. Despite the late hour, they could hear distant cars and sirens, their parents still arguing, faint music from a faraway radio, and the electric hum of power lines above.

"Why do they have to fight like this?" Gennie wondered aloud.

"Did you hear what they said? We're going to have to move. They've got to sell our house." Jeff was upset.

"I don't want to move away," Gennie replied.

"This is the worse they've ever fought," Jeff observed. "Mom told me they might live away from each other."

"I know. Dad gave me the big talk about that, too," Gennie said sadly. "All they ever fight about is money."

"Gennie, they had money but they lost it or something. That's why they always yell at each other. Now we're going to have to move."

"It's not fair. Why can't we be rich?" Gennie asked wistfully.

"Yea, right, Gennie. That's impossible," Jeff said. He sounded discouraged. They stared glumly into the soft night, feeling helpless.

It was Jeff who saw it first. He stiffened and leaned forward, squinting. Far down the street, barely within sight, something was moving. Something was moving very, very slowly close to the ground.

"Gennie, what's that?" Jeff asked pointing.

"I don't know. It looks like fog or something," Gennie replied.

The slowly advancing layer of mist, only a few inches above the ground, appeared silver-white in the bright moonlight, and was almost fluorescent against the night. As the silver mist slithered ever

3

so slowly down the street, it spread into driveways, up across yards, and smothered the ground everywhere. It was like a strange ghost-like serpent moving in slow motion.

"That is weird," Jeff said.

"Creepy," Gennie agreed.

It swirled around the base of telephone poles, street signs, the buildings, and the cars parked along the street. Like an ocean tide, it continued moving toward the Douglas house, gradually swallowing everything in its path. Jeff and Gennie watched wide-eyed as it advanced closer and closer toward their house. It crept through their chain link fence, slithered across the small yard, and swirled around the bottom porch step. They watched in fascination as it continued past their house to the end of the street, until the entire block was shrouded in the mysterious apparition.

Gennie edged back from the bottom step, somewhat frightened of the ghost-like fog, but Jeff ventured off the porch and stepped right into the mist. It came up to his knees.

"Gennie, come down here," Jeff urged his sister. "It's cool! Walk into it. It's just fog or something."

Jeff began walking back and forth, making the mist swirl around him and rise up above his head. When he stopped moving, it quickly fell back to earth, determined to hug the ground in a thick coating. Jeff again called for his sister to join him, but Gennie was listening to something else.

"Jeff, shhhh," Gennie said abruptly. "Listen."

"What?" Jeff said in a loud voice.

"Shhh!"

"What is it?" Jeff asked in a loud whisper.

"Listen. Just listen," Gennie instructed him.

Jeff stopped jumping about and listened to the night.

"I don't hear anything," Jeff said, confused by his sister's insistence.

"That's the point. There's no sound at all, Jeff. Absolutely nothing."

Sure enough, the night was quieter than they'd ever remembered. No sounds of faraway cars, no humming of power transformers overhead, no chattering of distant television sets or radios, and no sirens across the city. Even their parents' bitter quarreling had stopped. The city was deathly still.

"Oh my gosh!" Gennie exclaimed.

"What is it?" Jeff asked.

"My watch," Gennie said. "The display has frozen. It just keeps flashing 2:03. It's broken or something." Jeff was becoming more concerned, and cautiously stepped out of the mist, back to the porch steps. For a few moments, all they could hear was the pounding of their own hearts.

"What was that?" Jeff asked, looking about. Gennie cocked her head to one side and listened intently. She could hear it, too. Far off, several streets away, they could hear a faint tapping followed by a small tinkling sound, like a tiny bell. Then they heard it again, and again. Each tap was followed by tinkling. Each tinkling was followed by tapping. It continued in a slow methodical rhythm. Tap–tinkle–tap–tinkle–tap–tinkle. The sound was faint but becoming louder. Tap–tinkle–tap–tinkle. It was getting closer!

"Whatever it is, it's coming this way," Jeff said in a barely audible whisper.

"Shhhh," Gennie said.

They could hear it clearly now, and straining their eyes, they could make out a figure of some sort, far off at the end of the street. The figure was walking slowly through the mist toward the Douglas house carrying a long stick or staff with a tiny bell attached to it. With each step, the staff was planted on the ground, making the tapping sound.

Gennie and Jeff took a step back, making a quick escape into the house more possible if necessary. The figure drew closer. They could see now that it was a peculiarly dressed old man. Very calmly, and apparently in no particular hurry, the man turned into the Douglas yard and walked right up to the porch steps. He stopped, and looked up at Gennie and Jeff.

The little man was most curious. He was no taller than Gennie and clearly very old. He had a thick head of snow-white hair, somewhat wild and a bit too long. His face was a weather-beaten mass of crevasses and wrinkles, as if toughened from countless years in the sun. It looked like dried jerky. His eyes were an odd olive-green, but surprisingly bright and alert for someone of such an age. With just a slight smile on his lips, he appeared calm and serene. It was not an expression one often encountered in the city.

His clothes were the most curious of all. He was dressed as in ancient times, in robes and a tunic of rough-looking cloth. Around his waist, a strand of rope held a small leather drawstring pouch. The hand with which he clutched his staff was as brown and wrinkled as his face. Upon noting he wore unusual sandals on his feet, Gennie and Jeff realized the mist did not cover his feet as it had Jeff's, but swirled around and away from his feet as he walked. He was the one thing the mist seemed to avoid.

"What do you want?" Gennie asked.

"What do I want?" The old man chuckled with a warm smile. "Why, I don't want anything. I'm here because of what you want."

"I think you must want somebody else. Are you lost?" Jeff asked.

"Oh, I don't think so, Gennie and Jeff Douglas," the old man said.

Gennie and Jeff exchanged surprised glances. They weren't sure what to make of the stranger.

"What did you mean what I want?" Gennie asked.

"Didn't you say you wanted to be rich?" he asked.

"How did you know that?" Gennie asked, curiosity overtaking her fear.

"Oh, I know a great many things," the visitor said kindly. "I know that money is tearing apart your family. I know that you may have to move out of your home."

"Have you been hiding and listening to us? How long have you been out here?" Jeff demanded.

"Why, I've been here many years. I've been waiting for this exact moment in time for thirteen years," he answered calmly.

"Thirteen years? That's how old I am," Gennie observed.

"Yes, that's right," he said.

"There's nothing wrong with wanting to be rich," Jeff said.

"Wrong? On the contrary. That's exactly why I'm here," the old man smiled as he spoke.

"Why should we trust you?" Jeff questioned.

"Look around you, Jeff." The old man swept his arm to encompass the world. "I've stopped everything else, all around you, everywhere, because of how important this is. There's not a dog barking or a cat meowing, not a noise from a car or siren; your parents' voices are quiet. Everything, even time itself, has stopped."

"Who are you?" Gennie asked.

"Well, I think it best if the two of you call me Mr. Mortimer," the visitor replied.

"Mr. Mortimer," Jeff absently repeated. "So are you like a guardian angel?"

"Not really, but I am here to help you, or I should say, to help you two help yourselves," he added. "Come down here so I may speak with you."

Hesitantly, Gennie and Jeff stepped off the porch and into the yard to stand face to face with Mr. Mortimer.

"Are you going to make us rich?" Jeff asked hopefully.

"In a way. I'm going to teach you about wealth," he answered.

Jeff looked crestfallen. "Oh, great," he said sarcastically. "A lecture! I can get that from my dad."

"Oh, much more than just a lecture," the little man confided. "You do want to help your parents, don't you? And save your home?"

Gennie gave an enthusiastic, "Yes!"

"There are three secrets to acquiring wealth. They are called the Three Pillars. The Three Pillars are secrets the ancients have handed down from one generation to the next."

"Why don't you just make us rich if you want to help us?" Jeff asked.

"I am here to *really* help you. This isn't make-believe, Jeff. It's not about digging up pirate treasure," he said, looking toward Jeff. "And it's not about winning the lottery," he said to Gennie. "This is about how real people acquire wealth. Only by learning and understanding the Three Pillars of Wealth, can you save your home, and your parents. Do you understand?"

Both Gennie and Jeff nodded solemnly.

"When do you want us to start?" Gennie asked.

"Now," Mr. Mortimer replied.

CHAPTER 2

The Chamber of Pillars

Jeff and Gennie found themselves standing upon marble steps leading to a huge stone building. The building had the appearance of a Greek Temple, but much, much larger—perhaps ten stories high, rising one hundred feet from its base, with a huge domed roof at its summit. Below the children were several hundred steps leading up to the structure.

As they looked down the long set of stairs, they realized the ancient building was perched on a hilltop overlooking a vast desert. All around them, to the end of every horizon, was an endless ocean of sand. Before them stretched rolling dune after rolling dune with no signs of life; a barren wasteland.

It was then they noticed the heat. In the brief time they stood on the steps, they began to suffer under the sun's searing intensity. The stifling heat radiated off the stone steps. Their lungs burned with each difficult breath.

"Let's move inside," Mr. Mortimer said. "Too long under this sun and you'll soon look like me."

The kids smiled and the old man laughed aloud. They walked up the few remaining steps to the base of the structure and entered a narrow, darkly lit doorway that led inside to the temple's central chamber. They followed the downward sloping passageway for a few minutes to where the dark cool air inside was a welcome relief from the oppressive heat outside.

The narrow passageway finally opened into a magnificent, cavernous chamber, larger than any room Gennie or Jeff had ever stood in. The circular-shaped hall was at least three hundred feet across from one curved wall to another. The ceiling rose to a dizzying height. The walls had no decorations—no paintings, no statues, no windows. The only adornments were small metal oil lamps every ten feet. Although there were dozens of these lamps, their flickering flames were not bright enough to fully light the huge room so the center of the hall and most of the ceiling were hidden in shadows. The floor was an intricate mosaic of tiny hexagonal tiles, meticulously and individually laid centuries ago. So perfect was the hall's design that the slightest noise, the softest footstep or the quietest whisper, echoed throughout the chamber.

In the center of the vast chamber stood three colossal pillars, monstrous sentinels that rose the full height of the ceiling, and towered over the visitors. Like giant redwoods, the columns spanned nearly seventy feet in diameter and were so tall that they disappeared into the darkness above.

Jeff and Gennie gazed up in awe at the tremendous structures.

"You now stand before the Three Pillars of Wealth," Mr. Mortimer said with a proud smile.

Gennie and Jeff touched the smooth stone at the base of one of the giant columns. The stone was cool to the touch, like the rest of the chamber. Gennie glanced at her hand. It was dark with soot and grime.

"They're filthy," she exclaimed, looking for some place to wipe her hands. Jeff wiped his on his pants.

"Gennie, don't be such a neat-freak," her brother said.

"Why is everything here so dirty?" Gennie asked.

"The pillars have stood here for thousands of years, and receive few visitors. Very few of late," the old man surmised.

"So what happens now?" Jeff asked.

"Each pillar holds a secret to obtain wealth. To understand their secrets, you must learn about them in order," Mr. Mortimer said.

"So we need to find the First Pillar," Gennie said.

"Yes. Your journey will begin with the first," Mr. Mortimer replied.

Gennie immediately began searching around the pillar which had a small numeral "I" outlined in red in the floor.

"There's nothing here! I thought there might be some carved words, even in code or something," Gennie complained. "But it's blank. It's just a pillar."

"The Pillars of Wealth will not reveal themselves to you unless you already know their secrets," Mr. Mortimer cryptically explained.

"But that doesn't make sense," Gennie said, circling the pillar again. "If we knew the secret, we wouldn't care about the pillar."

"Is this some sort of riddle or trick?" Jeff asked.

Mr. Mortimer was not the least bit ruffled by the children's insistent questioning.

"You must first discover what each pillar represents," he said. "You must learn for yourselves what each of the Three Pillars of Wealth are. There is no other way."

"How do we do that?" Jeff asked.

"For each pillar, you shall take a short journey to another time and place. A quest. After you have successfully completed each journey, you shall return here to this chamber, and each pillar will reveal its secret to you," Mr. Mortimer said.

"All right. We can do that," Gennie replied confidently.

"No sweat," Jeff added. "Let's get going!"

"But I must warn you first," Mr. Mortimer said. His tone was serious. "Once you venture back in search of each pillar's truth, I cannot help you. You will be entirely on your own. The secret will be somewhere in your midst. Thoughtfully observe the words and deeds of all those around you. The secret will be there for you to find. You will have just three days to recognize each secret."

Mr. Mortimer paused and looked directly at them. "It is very important you understand—no more than three days for each journey."

"And if we don't discover one of the pillars, or the secret, do we end up back home, in our front yard, just as we left it?" Jeff inquired of the old man.

"You must discover each pillar in order. The First, then the Second, and finally the Third Pillar," Mr. Mortimer said, avoiding Jeff's question. "You must complete them all. Ignoring even one of the pillars will make wealth as elusive as a rainbow. A mirage you can never grasp."

"But if we can't find one of the secrets, are we back home?"

Jeff insisted.

Mr. Mortimer was slow to answer. He looked quietly upon the two for what seemed an uncomfortably long time before answering.

"I'm afraid if you do not discover the secret, or the pillar of wealth to be found in that journey, you cannot return," he said solemnly.

"What!" Gennie stammered, not believing she heard correctly.

"Ever? What do you mean? That's crazy!" Jeff announced.

"The opportunity to learn the secrets of the Three Pillars exacts a heavy toll," he continued. "There can be no turning back, no quitting, no giving up when the situation becomes difficult. You are expected to discover the Pillars of Wealth. Between journeys, you can quit if you choose to. But when you're within the journey itself, you must find the answer. There is no other way."

Gennie still doubted the finality of the old man's words.

"But, I mean, everybody comes back safely, right? You wouldn't get us into something really dangerous would you? You just want us to try our best," she said.

"I sincerely hope your best will be good enough," he replied.

"So are you saying it is dangerous?" Jeff asked.

Again Mr. Mortimer paused. Looking upon Gennie and Jeff with sad eyes, he said, "I'm afraid there are many who have not come back, and who never will."

His words sent a cold chill through both of them.

"Decide now if you wish to continue. Once you begin, there is no turning back."

"If we do this," Gennie asked, "and we discover the Three Pillars of Wealth, will we be able to save our family for sure?"

They both looked hopefully at the old man.

"I cannot answer that," he said. "I cannot foretell the future. But I do know that once you understand the pillars, you will have the knowledge to attain wealth. And you will be able to share that knowledge with your mother and father. Would that not help them?"

There was a long pause as Gennie and Jeff thought about their choices.

"Oh, heck, let's do it, Gennie!" Jeff blurted out. "We don't really have anything to lose!"

"Okay, I guess it can only help," she agreed. Gennie turned to Mr. Mortimer. "We're in! Let's go!"

Mr. Mortimer smiled. "I have great confidence in both of you. Your first task will be to uncover the First Pillar. It is the most important pillar of the three. From the First Pillar, all else flows. Good luck."

Mr. Mortimer gave a peculiar wave of his hand, and a column of fluorescent mist encircled Gennie and Jeff. As it spun upward toward the sky, Gennie and Jeff disappeared.

THE
FIRST PILLAR

CHAPTER 3

The Barrier
of Stone

As the shimmering light faded, Gennie and Jeff saw a gigantic stone wall that dominated the landscape. The wall, which stood twenty-five feet high and almost as thick, was constructed of massive stone blocks, each the size of a refrigerator. The barrier ran in a straight line for about a quarter mile before it curved around a hillside and out of sight. This was a structure intended to stand forever.

In its entirety, the stone barrier was nearly three miles long, completely surrounding a large city of sun-dried brick buildings. Because this portion of the wall was not intended as an entrance into the city, there was no gate, doorway, or any break whatsoever. At this section, the wall had but one pur-pose—to keep out invading armies.

As formidable as this obstacle appeared, several hundred work-ers, mostly men, swarmed around it, building it higher still, fortify-ing it with one giant stone block after another, to increase the structure's height.

Crude scaffolding against portions of the wall crawled with workman filling cracks with small stones and mortar. A long, gradual ramp, nearly 150 yards long, ran next to the wall where it was being raised. The huge stones were pushed by brute manpower up the long ramp to the top of the wall. Once atop the wall, stone masons positioned the huge blocks into their final resting places.

Pushing the stones up the long ramp was grueling work. It took four or five men two full hours to move one stone from the base of the ramp to the top of the wall. Because of the tremendous effort required, and the intensity of the sun overhead, the workmen were drenched in sweat.

That was the second thing Gennie and Jeff noticed—it was hot. The landscape was dry and arid. It wasn't painfully scorching heat like they experienced outside the temple of the Three Pillars, but it was much, much hotter than they were accustomed to.

The builders, foremen, and stone masons wore knee-length white tunics with leather sandals. The workmen performing the most physically demanding work were stripped to the waist.

Jeff was the first to break the silence. "Where are we?" he said, looking about the large work area.

"I've no idea," Gennie said in wonder. "We're really back in time. Way back in time!"

"It looks like Greek or Roman or something like that," Jeff guessed. His conclusion was based less on history books and more on period movies he had seen. Gennie was the first to notice Mr. Mortimer had sent them back in time with some minor changes.

"Look at our clothes," she said. The two were dressed in the same white loose-fitting tunics worn by all the other children in camp. Crude leather sandals had replaced their shoes.

"This thing makes me look fat," Gennie complained.

"Gennie will you chill out? Who cares what you look like back here?"

"I do," she said, pulling at the poorly fitting garment.

"What now?" Jeff asked his older sister when she stopped fussing with her clothing.

"I don't know. I'm not even sure what we're looking for," she announced.

"We need to find someone who has lots of money," Jeff concluded. "That should be the starting point. Then we find out how they got it. It may be easier than we think."

"Maybe," Gennie said thoughtfully, not believing for a moment that any of this would be easy.

A large field separated this section of the wall from the farthest outskirts of the city. Upon the field was a city of tents, more than one hundred of them, temporary homes of the workers and their families. The encampment was bustling with small children and toddlers running about. The women not directly involved in the construction of the wall were preoccupied with household chores. Whereas the men's and children's tunics were white, the women wore bright colors, including yellow, blue, and purple. The women's tunics, much more modest than the men's, reached the ground, so even their feet were covered.

A loud voice interrupted Gennie's and Jeff's thoughts.

"You there, why are you standing about? There's work to be

done!" A man approached, walking with an air of authority. Like most of the men in the camp, he had dark features and wore a thick beard. His face was punctuated by extremely pronounced cheekbones. Although his tunic had once been white, it was now a dull gray, discolored from day after day of grime and sweat.

"You two are new to this site," he correctly observed.

Gennie and Jeff nervously glanced at each other, concerned that somehow this man knew they were from another time and place.

"Your tunics; they are the cleanest I have seen in some time," the man said with a keen eye. "And your hands; they are not accustomed to hard work."

Gennie and Jeff instinctively looked down at their clean, smooth hands. The man's sharp eye missed little. By comparison, the man's hands were dirty and scraped. Many of his fingers were crooked and bent from being broken, more than once. His forearms were covered with small scars.

"No matter!" he said. "All hands are welcome here. If you are not accustomed to hard work, you soon shall be. In a week's time, you'll be proud of the calluses you've earned."

He extended an open hand for the children to view. His palm was covered with thick leather-like calluses, testimony to a lifetime of hard physical work.

"What are your names?" he asked the children.

"My name is Gennie Douglas," Gennie answered.

"I'm Jeff Douglas, Gennie's brother."

"Curious names. I am Truit the Taskmaster. I am in charge of this work site." He looked Gennie and Jeff over carefully, as if examining a piece of fruit he might buy in the market. "You are too old to run errands like the smaller children, but not old enough to work the stones." He thought for a moment, appraising their potential.

"You shall sweep the ramp ahead of the stones as they are pushed up the ramp to the wall. The ramp must be kept free of broken pieces of rock and wood. A smooth surface makes the stones move easier. Collect some bushes and clear the ramp, staying ahead of the stones. Do you understand?" Truit asked.

"Yes," Gennie and Jeff both answered.

"Good!" Truit pointed out a man near the wall who was supervising a group of workers. "Tell him you have spoken with me. He will show you where to work."

"Soldiers approaching!" someone shouted.

Several hundred yards away, a column of mounted soldiers galloped hard toward the encampment. One by one, the workers looked up and halted their work to watch the advancing column, setting down their tools. All progress on the huge blocks stopped. Women clung to their small children.

The soldiers were an impressive sight. Dust billowed up around the thirty riders whose polished bronze helmets and shields gleamed under the bright sun. Their red tunics and capes were in brilliant contrast to the desolate and dreary countryside. Each soldier carried a long lance or spear along with his shield, and a short sword at his waist.

Here was the pride of the city; a small portion of the proud and fierce army that had defended the city for so long.

The riders entered the work area and brought their horses to a stop. The soldier at the head of the column wore no helmet, and all could see his features. As the workers and their families recognized this man, a murmur raced through camp.

"It is Hector!" was whispered, and "Hector himself." "Behold it is Hector, the greatest of all the warriors!"

What had originally been simple curiosity about the soldier's approach gave way to fascination, and now to reverence. The workers farthest away strained on tiptoes to see this man. Women, who had hidden their children, lifted them in their arms so that they might remember the day they caught sight of this great warrior. The mothers whispered to their children, "Look, it is Hector!"

Hector, leader of the city's army, was its bravest and greatest warrior. His exploits on the battlefield had become legendary and the stuff of stories and songs. The entire encampment was in hushed awe that so great a warrior, whose name was spoken in tones normally reserved for the gods, had come to visit this far corner of the city.

Gennie and Jeff were no more than fifteen feet from the famous commander. Since he stayed upon his horse, it was difficult to tell his height, but he was clearly stronger than the other soldiers. Hector's arms were solid, battle-hardened sinew and muscle. When Hector looked in the direction of Gennie and Jeff, they understood that here was the fiercest of soldiers. They could see it in his eyes, which burned with an intensity, savageness, and fearlessness they had never seen before. It was a little frightening.

The great soldier spurred his horse to where Truit the Taskmaster stood. Truit rushed to the horse's side and gave a slight bow of his head in reverence.

"I am Truit, the taskmaster of this far section of the city's wall. We are greatly honored by your presence. You shall inspire us to work even harder to defend our city," Truit said, looking up in adulation to the mounted figure.

"I was told to find you, Truit. I have a message from the king for these citizens," Hector said in deep voice, looking out over the camp. "With your leave, I will address them."

"Please do so," Truit replied.

Both Hector and Truit knew the request was a mere formality. If the king wished Hector to address the workers, it would happen whether Truit wished it or not.

"Citizens!" Hector called out to the hundreds of workers and laborers clustered around the soldiers. "I bring you word from King Paris. It is now the seventh year in which our city has been under siege. We have learned that the Greeks have sent a fleet of ships with yet more soldiers. I believe they shall attempt to attack, rather than wait any longer for us to give out.

"It is for this reason we must raise the walls even higher, and why citizens from throughout the city, such as yourselves, are aiding the fortification of our defenses. As you know, King Paris has pledged that for each great stone that a team of men place atop the wall, that team shall share one silver stater!"

At this, the crowded camp murmured its approval.

"A most generous offer," Truit said. "These are all good citizens who would gladly help defend the city without such a reward. But by offering such a prize, King Paris shows both generosity and wisdom."

Hector continued, "Because of the approaching fleet, we must ask you to work even harder, to raise the height of the wall as rapidly as possible."

Hector stopped and scanned the workers. His nearby lieutenant handed him a clay tablet. Hector read it quickly, then returned it.

"Where is the man named Caltor, who is called 'Caltor the Colossus'?" All eyes in the camp looked about and fixed upon a group of men sitting on the ground.

"Rise to your feet, Caltor!" the Taskmaster called out.

Slowly, one of the men stood. Gennie and Jeff were amazed as he did so. Caltor was truly a colossus! He was a mountain of a man, standing nearly two heads taller than the other men around him. His giant shoulders and arms were like those of a great bear. His legs were like the stumps of mighty oak trees protruding from under his great belly. His hands were enormous.

"Caltor, I have been told you have the strength of four men, and can push one of the great stones in place single-handed," Hector called out.

"That is true, Hector," the giant man answered in a booming voice. "None of the workers are as mighty as myself."

"He speaks the truth," the Taskmaster said. "If we had more men with the strength of Caltor, this wall would be raised in a matter of days!"

"Your strength is well-known, Caltor," Hector said, praising the giant in front of all the other workers. "You are fortunate. When this wall is complete, the only weight you will be carrying will be a heavy purse of silver!" The other workers laughed at this, and the men closest to Caltor slapped him on the back approvingly.

"King Paris bestows his gratitude upon you all, and urges the greatest haste."

Hector paused, and looked about the sea of faces, many of whom looked to Hector to find their own courage.

"We will never let the Greeks overrun our city. I vow to you that they will never enter our city's gates! We will prevail!"

The workers and their families cheered Hector's words. Hector thanked the Taskmaster, gave a slight wave to the crowd, and rode off with his troops in search of the next building site along the wall.

Gennie and Jeff watched as the soldiers rode out of sight.

"Did you hear that, Jeff?" Gennie asked.

"About the war?" Jeff said.

"No, about the money. Each group gets to share one silver coin for each of those huge blocks they put in place on the wall," she said. "But that Caltor doesn't need any help to do it. He can do it alone and won't have to share the money with anyone else."

"You're right!" Jeff said, understanding what his sister was getting at. "Of all the workers here, he'll make way more than anyone else."

"A lot more than anyone else!" Gennie added.

"That sure sounds like the first step in becoming rich," Jeff said. "It looks like Caltor will lead us to the First Pillar of Wealth!"

CHAPTER 4

Caltor the Colossus

Gennie and Jeff collected brush from the nearby hillside with which to sweep the ramp. The two agreed that working alongside the others in camp would allow them to ask questions without creating a great deal of suspicion.

Even before reaching the work site, Gennie and Jeff could see a crowd of men had gathered. When they were closer, they saw that one of the large stone blocks had fallen off the sled-like device used to drag the stones from the quarry. This particular block was a corner piece, and, as such, was much larger than the normal refrigerator-size blocks.

Four men were trying to turn the block back over, to get it into position for its eventual slow journey up the ramp. The other workers crowded around, angrily blaming one another for the problem they now faced. Truit the Taskmaster, trying to maintain order, called to Gennie and Jeff.

"You two climb atop the ramp and be ready to clear a path for this stone. Once it is righted, we will begin pushing it up to the wall. I want nothing to halt its progress!" he said.

The four men rocked the massive piece back and forth, but it wouldn't quite turn over, although the men came close to tilting it back onto its base.

Then the men turned to see a huge figure swaggering through the crowd. It was Caltor. Still flush with Hector's praise, Caltor intended to show the entire camp how great his strength really was. He stopped in front of the large corner block.

"Stand back," he told the other workers. They released their grip, and the block fell back onto its side with a heavy thud. The workers, unsure whether they should abandon their efforts, looked to Truit for direction.

"Do as he says," Truit confirmed. "Caltor knows his own strength better than anyone here."

The workers backed away. By now, many of the other workers had halted their individual tasks and had gathered in a large circle around Caltor and the toppled stone. Caltor reached down, firmly grasped the lower edge of the great block, and, straining mightily, tilted one side of the stone as high as the four men had been able to move it. With a second effort, he raised it higher still, until the stone toppled back onto its base.

The workers who had gathered gave a cheer and slapped Caltor on his massive back in congratulations. The greater challenge, of course, was to move the oversized stone up the ramp, where the stone masons waited. Truit began assembling a team to push the massive piece to where it was needed, high above their heads.

"You six," Truit said, pointing to a group of workers. "Your backs look strong. We'll need all of you to get this corner piece atop the wall. I want four of you behind the stone to push, while you two push from the sides. That will keep it moving straight. We can't have this piece tumbling off the ramp. Sweepers, are you ready?"

Gennie and Jeff nodded, a little worried they were suddenly part of such an important work effort. But Caltor interrupted the men as they began to position themselves around the stone.

"This is my stone, Truit. I alone will take it up the ramp," Caltor said in a quiet yet determined voice. A number of the surrounding workers smiled to themselves. Caltor had finally bitten off more than even he could chew.

"Caltor, even your great strength is not equal to the task of so great a stone. Wait for the next block, it is of a more common size," Truit suggested. "No one will think less of you for passing on this."

"Do you doubt my strength?" Caltor asked Truit.

"Never, but every man has his limits, even you. I would hate to see you hurt when there are many here who together can do the work," Truit replied.

"Then it is time this entire camp learned of Caltor's true strength," Caltor said in a loud voice.

The workers moved back to give the giant more room. Some of the women and children from the tent city had begun to congregate behind the workers, anxious to see what was occurring.

"All right, Caltor, you shall have your chance," Truit said. "Clear away all persons from beneath the ramp. Sweepers, stay as close to the stone as possible. I want not a grain of sand or a sliver of wood to hamper the stone."

Truit turned to Caltor and placed a hand upon the huge man's shoulder. "Good luck, my friend. May the gods add to your great strength."

Caltor positioned himself behind the large corner stone, wedged his giant shoulder against its edge, and solidly planted his feet. He pushed against the stone with all his might, using his great legs, back, and arms in unison. Caltor's huge legs shook. His face grew red. The veins stood out upon his huge neck.

Almost the entire camp of two hundred people had halted all activities to watch. The stone was so large, even for Caltor, that all thought here was finally a task greater than the man. Many thought a public failure might finally curb his conceit.

Rivulets of perspiration trickled down Caltor's arms and brow. His face grew even redder. But the stone wouldn't budge. Then, ever so slightly, it moved. At first just an inch, then a few more inches, then a bit more until Caltor was able to take half a step forward. Again it moved, this time half a foot, and Caltor stepped forward again. The huge stone was moving! Slowly, painstakingly, the great corner piece inched upward. The camp was spellbound. Everyone held his or her breath as one. This was a remarkable feat. Could the giant move the stone the full distance up the ramp?

Perspiration now poured off Caltor, but the stone was moving faster. He drove the massive block up the ramp slowly but steadily. In front, Genie and Jeff swept furiously. All eyes were riveted on Caltor, and thus also on Gennie and Jeff. If a small rock or a tiny pebble slowed Caltor's momentum the slightest amount, they would be to blame.

The camp watched in absolute silence. Time passed agonizingly slowly. The only sounds were the swishing of the children's brooms, and Caltor's straining breath.

After ten minutes, Caltor was halfway up the ramp. His tremendous effort under the hot sun left pools of perspiration in each of his footsteps. Sweat rained off his huge torso.

As the awestruck onlookers began to realize Caltor was nearing the top, they began to chant his name. They called to him in encouragement. Even normally subdued Truit urged him onward.

Finally, Caltor and the stone reached the top of the ramp. The camp erupted in cheers. Surely, they had witnessed a miracle. Surely, this was a sign from the gods that their city would be protected. Caltor fell to one knee, utterly exhausted by his effort. The stone masons atop the wall shook their heads in disbelief.

Although no notice was made of the two new sweepers who had carefully cleared the way for Caltor, they, too, were exhausted and bathed in sweat. Gennie and Jeff were worn out from the effort and the pressure of knowing that, in a small sense, Caltor had been dependent upon them. The two smiled with relief. Not only had they successfully reached the top of the ramp, but they also were convinced that they were on the right track to the First Pillar of Wealth.

A man who could move a stone such as this surely would earn an enormous sum of silver staters each day he worked. Gennie and Jeff thought they would soon pass the first test Mr. Mortimer had put before them.

CHAPTER 5

Trapped in Time

Gennie and Jeff stopped for lunch later than the other children in the camp. They waited in a long line for a large piece of bread and a small bit of bitter white cheese. They found a shady spot to rest, apart from the other workers. Most of the encampment crowded under the large food tent where a woman with dark hair walked amongst them pouring water from a large gourd into outstretched wooden cups. Gennie and Jeff waited for her to approach them, thirsty from the morning's activities under the hot sun.

The two chose this particular spot because they could easily watch Caltor. Caltor came in for lunch much earlier than the other workers.

And now, having finished a massive lunch, rather than return to work, he played with the children in the camp. He let them climb upon him, as if he were a giant tree, and then carefully he shook them off, much to the children's squealing delight. Or he would lift a child in each hand high over his head, so they might receive a grand view of the camp. The children jumped about, calling his name, hoping they would be the next to be hoisted high overhead.

Over the course of the morning, Gennie and Jeff watched Caltor. They noticed that ever since Hector had praised his great strength, the giant had not accomplished much. Immediately after Hector and the soldiers departed, Caltor had pushed the large corner piece up the ramp, without any help, to the wild cheers of the other workers. Even Gennie and Jeff had to marvel at this huge man's incredible strength.

But then Caltor just stood around, watching four fellow workers struggle and strain to push another great stone up the ramp into place. Gennie calculated that Caltor had earned a silver stater for a single fifteen-minute effort, while it took four men almost two hours to do the same. In the two hours it had taken the four men to move the block, Caltor could have pushed eight blocks up the ramp! And Caltor didn't have to split his silver staters four ways. So while it would take a normal man eight hours to earn one silver stater, in that same time Caltor could earn thirty-two!

Surely, this was Mr. Mortimer's first secret to wealth. In a matter of days, Caltor would have a full pouch of silver coins. If the work lasted a month…Gennie couldn't do the math fast enough. But both Gennie and Jeff agreed that Caltor would be the wealthiest man in the entire camp before long.

Yet now, in the early afternoon, as the shadows began to lengthen, Caltor still had only pushed one block up the ramp to the stone masons. Most of the other men continued their hard labor through-out the day. Gennie could see that by day's end, unless Caltor went back to the scaffolding work area, he would finish the day with no more money, perhaps even less, than the smaller men around him.

Caltor was now ignoring the children, as some of the older girls came over to flirt with him. Caltor was clearly enjoying his new-found popularity and seemed in no hurry to return to the hot and dirty work area.

"I wish he would get back to work," Gennie said, trying to chew the tough bread without anything to drink. "He's already wasted half the day. He won't earn very much by talking to those girls."

"But he's already earned one piece of silver," Jeff said in support of Caltor. "All he has to do is push a few more blocks up the ramp. He'll still wind up with more money than anyone else here."

"I suppose so. We need to follow him around and watch every-thing he does," Gennie said quietly, as the woman with the water approached. "There may be other things he does that are impor-tant, besides being so strong. He's the only clue we have to the First Pillar."

The thin woman with dark hair offered Genie and Jeff some of the refreshing water. But when she heard Gennie say "First Pillar," the gourd fell from her hands and broke upon the ground. The woman lurched forward and seized Gennie by the shoulders, grip-ping her tightly. Gennie struggled a bit, but the woman seemed uncommonly strong.

"The First Pillar! Did you say the First Pillar?" The woman be-came wide-eyed, her voice strained and desperate. "Speak to me, you little fool! Did you say the First Pillar?" She shook Gennie.

"Yes," Gennie managed to say. The woman stopped shaking Gennie. Her face, now only a few inches from Gennie's, was pale.

"You're not from here, are you? I've never seen you before! Answer me! Did Mr. Mortimer send you? Did he? Are you here to discover the First Pillar?" the woman now spoke in a pleading, whining voice.

Jeff grabbed one of her hands and pulled hard, to break her hold on Gennie. It worked. Gennie immediately backed away beyond her grasp.

"Take me with you, please!" the woman begged both of them. "I don't belong here. Mortimer sent me here four years ago. Four years!" she screeched in her raspy voice. "He gave me three days to discover the secret of the First Pillar. Three days is nothing! How was I to find out anything in only three days? It was impossible. Nothing but a cruel trick."

Several workers near the large tent looked over to see if everything was all right. The woman's ravings had not gone unnoticed. The woman lowered her voice to a whisper, but it had the same undercurrent of utter desperation.

"Have you discovered the First Pillar?" she looked to the two children hopefully.

"Not yet," Jeff announced. "But we think..."

"No!" Gennie cut him off. "We don't know what the First Pillar is."

"Ah, so you're guarding your little secret, are you? Don't want to take Sarah back with you, is that it?" the water-carrier asked.

"I don't think we can take anyone back with us," Gennie answered honestly.

"Lies!" she shouted back at Gennie and Jeff.

Several of the workers at the tent called to the woman. "Water! Get over here woman and bring us water! We've been working all morning."

The nearly crazed woman looked over her shoulder toward the tent. "In a moment!" she screamed. She turned her attention back to Gennie and Jeff.

"How much time has the old wizard given you? A week? A month? Tell me!" she shrieked.

"He gave us three days," Jeff answered. "The same as you."

"What? Three days! He *is* mad. Three days is not enough time! I have been here four years. It has taken me that long to learn there is no secret of the First Pillar. Wealth is a matter of luck. It's impossible to discover something that does not exist. Mortimer has purposely trapped me in this backward world. I've had to steal, and beg, and now wait hand and foot on the likes of these," she said, gesturing to the camp of workers behind her.

"Water!" another voice called from the tent. However, this time it was Truit the Taskmaster, and the woman could not ignore her duties any longer.

"Coming," she called back reluctantly. She picked up the broken gourd and began to retreat.

"I'm not alone," she quietly said, addressing the children once more. "There are others like me. In three days time, you'll join us whether you like it or not. There is no escape from this terrible place. Mortimer has played a cruel hoax on all of us."

She turned and returned to the food tent to retrieve another gourd and begin her duties once more.

CHAPTER 6

False Hopes

During the afternoon, with the sun at its hottest, Gennie and Jeff were permitted to alternate with another team of young sweepers. The two Douglases escorted the slow procession of stone blocks up the ramp for an hour, frantically brushing all the while. They were then allowed to take an hour break, while three younger children temporarily took their place. This gave Gennie and Jeff time to rest, gather fresh brush for the makeshift brooms, and get plenty of water.

Throughout the afternoon, they anxiously awaited Caltor's return, in hopes that now being fully rested from his public demonstration in the morning, he would at least take five or six stones up to the top of the wall before the day's end. Even when they picked new brooms, one of them always kept an eye on the ramp for Caltor. But Caltor didn't return to the work area until dusk, at which time there was only half-an-hour left until quitting time.

Only then, at the very end of the day, did Caltor push one last stone block up the ramp. Unlike his performance in the morning, he appeared bored and somewhat reluctant about the whole business.

At the conclusion of each day, after the work was done and before dinner was prepared in the large community tent, all the workers lined up to receive their pay.

Gennie's earlier calculations were correct. Nearly all the men had been on small teams, to push the stones up the ramp—and nearly all the men received one silver stater for their day's work. When Caltor's name was announced, Jeff and Gennie leaned forward in anticipation. Caltor received only two silver staters. It was certainly better than the other men, but still a far cry from his potential. Caltor ambled off to the large tent for his supper with Gennie and Jeff following close behind.

After dinner, Jeff noticed Caltor and three of his fellow workers slip out of the food tent and head out across the large field.

"They're leaving." Jeff tugged at Gennie's tunic. "Let's follow them!"

"I'm not done yet. I'm only half done with my food!" she complained. Gennie usually ate much slower than Jeff did.

"Come on or we'll lose them," Jeff urged. Gennie gulped down a last bite and left the tent with Jeff.

The two ran quietly after the giant man and his friends. They watched as the four disappeared into a large tent at the far end of the field. Gennie and Jeff could see the shadows of many men sitting inside. Their flickering shadows were projected onto the tent walls from warm oil lamps burning inside.

Approaching quietly, Gennie and Jeff cautiously peeked through the slit in the two flaps that made the doorway. The tent was filled with a dozen workers sitting on large rocks, casks, and piles of sheepskins. The men were tightly crowded into the structure. The close quarters, after a hard day under the hot sun, made the air stuffy and pungent.

The men were drinking from large wooden cups. A short fat man with a bald head, whom the workers called Malkin, was wearing what appeared to be an apron. He squeezed himself about the crowded space refilling the men's cups as quickly as they emptied them. Caltor sat in the middle of the tent where the ceiling reached its highest point.

"Drink up, my friends," Malkin urged. "There is much more wine than this."

"Caltor's purse will allow us to drink all night," one of the men said. The entire tent erupted into laughter.

"Tonight you are all my friends, and we shall all share Malkin's wine," Caltor said in his booming voice, to the great merriment of the other men in the stuffy tent.

"I will drink the wine while Caltor pays," said one of the men. "But it is poor wine that Malkin pours."

"Then you have not had enough!" the short bald man replied with a grin.

"For the more of my wine you drink, the better it will taste."

Once again, all present roared with laughter.

"When I am done with this job, and this cursed siege is over, I'm going to buy a few goats," one of the men said to the others.

"That is nothing," another man boasted. "I plan to get a herd of goats. I'll sell the milk at a high price to all of your wives."

All the men in the tent laughed.

"A herd of goats is nothing," Caltor said. His booming voice commanded everyone's attention. "I will buy a caravan of camels, loaded with jewels and spices. If you are kind to me, I will let your herd of goats dine on the dung of my camels!"

Again the tent roared with laughter as the men drank more of Malkin's wine.

"Shall I open another cask of wine?" Malkin asked the group.

"Of course!" Caltor boomed, as he tossed the host a silver stater from his pouch. "With all these insects about me," he said, referring to his friends, "there is no wine left for a man of any size."

The men laughed, spurred on by Caltor's generosity.

"My camels will be the finest in the kingdom," Caltor continued. "And I shall have six or seven wives to keep me company on long journeys. I shall cover each wife in jewels from head to toe."

"And no land Caltor?" one of the men prodded him.

"Why, of course. I'll buy half the land in the city," Caltor said, draining yet another cup of wine. "Perhaps I'll buy King Paris's Royal Hall!"

"More wine?" Malkin asked. Half the men in the tent raised their cups. He rushed about filling them.

"You'll have to move every stone in the quarry to buy all that!" a worker from the far end of the tent called out to Caltor.

"And I shall," Caltor said. "Today the sun was too hot for hard work."

"Ah, but the day before you only moved one stone," another chimed in.

"I wanted to conserve my strength for a greater effort," Caltor answered.

"And the day before that?" the man asked. The laughter dried up. This last comment was close to an insult, and though the wine had dulled their senses, the men felt the tension. Luckily Malkin stepped in to defuse the situation.

"That was the day the women came by the wall on their way to the river. Would you prefer Truit's blocks of stone to the fairest flowers of the city?" Malkin said to the man who had spoken foolishly to Caltor. The men laughed, particularly Caltor, and the moment passed.

"If I wanted to, I could move a hundred of the great stones in a single day," Caltor boasted, "and one day I shall."

Caltor drank the wine in his cup and signaled for more.

"If you do, we will be able to bathe in wine tomorrow night," said one of the workers. All agreed with a great deal of laughter.

"Yes," Caltor said dreamily. "Someday I shall have a great caravan of camels, piled high with riches from afar. More wine for my friends! Let us drink to the caravan," he shouted, tossing Malkin his second silver stater.

"I've heard enough," Gennie quietly said. "I'm going back to the big tent."

"Those guys are sure drinking a lot," Jeff observed.

"Yes, and Caltor's paying for all of it," Gennie said angrily.

One of the women who cooked meals in the community tent had made up beds for Gennie and Jeff of sheepskins laid upon the ground with a thin wool blanket. The children were tired and dirty. The thick, soft skins looked very inviting. As they sat down on the skins, preparing to sleep for the night, Gennie spoke to an old man who was cleaning a pot nearby on his knees. "Excuse me. Do you know Caltor the Colossus?" she asked the man.

"Every man and woman in camp and throughout the city knows of Caltor," the man answered, glad to take a break from his scrubbing.

"Do you know how many stone blocks he normally pushes up the ramp each day?" Gennie inquired.

"Well now, not exactly. I'd say he always does one or two stones a day."

"One or two!" Gennie exclaimed, "Is that all?"

The old man laughed. "You seem disappointed. I would gladly trade places with him; anyone would. Think about it. He can do the work of many men in only a small portion of the time. In no time at all, he earns enough for food and plenty of drink, and he's a favorite of the girls," he said, winking to Jeff. "That's a good life indeed!"

"But he could do so much more!" Gennie said, becoming frustrated.

"But why should he?" the old man asked calmly. "He has everything he could want and has to work very little for it. I think every man in this camp would gladly trade places with Caltor."

The old man went back to his scrubbing. Gennie laid her head down on the thick wool.

"Great," she said sarcastically to Jeff. "This looks like a dead end."

Before long, the two were fast asleep, exhausted by the day's adventures. But Gennie was right to worry. One precious day had already slipped through their hands.

CHAPTER 7

Mortinas
the Elder

The next morning Truit the Taskmaster decided that all the children in the camp, who numbered about forty, would go to the field of ruins to gather loads of small stones and rock chips. Specifically, Truit sought small rectangular pieces that had broken off of old discarded monuments and blocks. These could then be inserted into the small cracks between the giant blocks in the wall to ensure stability as more of the massive stones were piled on top of one another. The field of ruins was a graveyard of stone where old boulders, broken columns, and portions of dismantled buildings were dumped.

Each child was given a straw basket with long straps. In this way, once the baskets were loaded with stone chips, the heavy load could be carried on the children's shoulders back to the wall where they were needed. The field of ruins was a quarter of a mile from the construction site at the wall. This was a good way for the youngest citizens to help in the city's defense.

Gennie and Jeff walked along the trail leading to the dump, just behind the others. As they walked to the ruins, they spoke with increasing concern about their situation, which was beginning to look somewhat bleak.

"This morning I overheard some of the workers talking about Caltor. They said he and the others spent all their money last night at that drinking place," Gennie said dejectedly. "This morning he's no better off than he was yesterday or the day before. And he won't be any better off tomorrow or the next day."

"I know. He talks about getting rich, but he's not doing anything about it," Jeff added. "I don't know what his problem is. He's so strong he could make more money than anyone!"

"If he worked harder he could spend all he wanted, and still have more than anyone else," Gennie observed.

"So now what?" Jeff asked, looking to his older sister for guidance. Jeff felt Gennie usually knew the right thing to do.

"I don't know. We're not going to learn anything about money from Caltor, and we wasted all of yesterday following him around. Now we only have two days left."

"We'll figure it out," Jeff said, trying to sound encouraging. "Mr. Mortimer wouldn't have sent us back here unless he thought we could solve it."

"Don't forget that Sarah woman from yesterday," Gennie

reminded Jeff. "Remember Mr. Mortimer warned us. We may not get back home!"

"We will," Jeff said. "We will!"

But in his heart, even Jeff began to worry that maybe Gennie was right, and that they wouldn't be able to solve the mysterious puzzle.

They arrived at the ruins. The large flat area of land, about the size of a football field, was littered with broken statues, broken columns, crushed monuments, and mounds of broken bits of white stone. Gennie and Jeff went to the far corner of the field, apart from where the other children were filling their baskets.

Jeff began to scoop debris into his basket from a small pile of rubble. As he removed the chips and shards, he uncovered an eerily familiar stone face.

"Gennie, come quick!" he shouted.

Gennie rushed to his side and looked down. There on the ground, surrounded by small rock bits, was the face of an old man with a hawk-like nose and peculiar eyes.

"It looks like," Gennie began.

"Mr. Mortimer," Jeff finished.

They frantically cleared away more of the rock bits. First just a head was revealed, then shoulders, then arms and legs. Soon they unearthed a huge statue, lying on its side, which was undoubtedly fashioned after Mr. Mortimer. By now, some of the other children had gathered to see what Gennie and Jeff had found. The statue had to be ten feet high when standing.

"It's him. It's exactly like him," Gennie said, as the two backed away to get better perspective.

"He looks exactly the same. His clothes, his staff, everything," Jeff said. "Look at his face. He has a slight smile."

Indeed, there could be no doubt. It was a perfect match. At one time, this huge likeness of Mr. Mortimer had perhaps adorned a building or temple, but now it lay in the dump, like so much garbage. As they gazed down at the monolith, not sure what to make of their discovery, a man approached.

"What have you found here?" he said to them.

"It's a statue of…" Jeff's voice froze as he looked up at the man.

The man was in his early 30s and wore a thick black beard. He carried a staff in his right hand, but his left arm ended in a scarred stump above the elbow. Startled, Jeff completely lost his train of thought.

"Don't be alarmed, boy," the man said. "I am Harton, Keeper of the Ruins. I lost my arm seven years ago at the beginning of the siege to Ajax himself."

"Ajax?" Gennie said, being careful not to stare at Harton's missing limb.

"Hard to believe? It was on the plains beyond the city. It was a pitched battle, and Ajax and I squared off. We exchanged blow for blow, each of us as skilled a swordsman as the other."

Harton became excited as he retold the story that he had told so many times to whomever would listen. "Then Ajax stumbled, and dropped his shield. He should have been mine!"

"What happened?" Jeff asked, much more intrigued by the tale than Gennie.

"The fates intervened," he said bitterly. "Ajax returned in glory, and I returned without an arm. I had but one chance to strike true, but I rushed my blow, and it merely glanced off his cursed helmet.

"Then the gods breathed the strength of ten into him. He rose and looked stronger, fresher, more powerful than ever before. He raised his sword," Harton said, raising his staff to illustrate his tale, "and struck a blow like no mortal alone could have struck. I could hear the metal singing through the air. I raised my shield, but to no avail. His sword sliced through my shield as if it were a reed. The same blow took my arm. Can a mere mortal fight a god?"

"No," Gennie answered.

Harton grew sullen. For a few moments, he was lost in thought, reliving his final battle for the thousandth time. No matter how many times he relived every blow and action of that struggle, the outcome was always the same.

"What have you found?" he finally said. "Aren't you gathering chips with the others for the wall?"

"Yes, but we found this statue," Gennie said, pointing to the huge figure lying on its side. "Do you know who it is?"

Harton looked down. "I've never seen it before," he said. "This must have been here for many, many years. It looks to be one of the ancient elders."

"Ancient elders? What do you mean?" Jeff asked.

"The ancient ones were the revered wise men who founded the city and this kingdom. They were honored for many years, long after their departure from the world of the living," he told them.

"What happened?" Gennie asked Harton.

"I know many of the elders were ignored as we learned of the gods," Harton said. "Since these men were mere mortals, it seemed foolish to honor them. But there was something different about this one. Some reason his likeness was torn down and destroyed."

"Do you remember this one?" Gennie asked him.

"I'm not sure," Harton said, rubbing his bearded chin. "I seem to remember something, but it was long ago. My grandfather used to tell me stories of the elders, but I was even younger than you when I heard them."

"Was his name Mr. Mortimer?" Jeff said to Harton, but looking at Gennie.

"Mortimer, Mortimer," Harton repeated, concentrating hard. "No, but that sounds close. Ah, that's it! Now I remember, it's Mortinas. He was the elder of abundance and plenty. The legend held that it was Mortinas who brought wealth and riches to the kingdom, but as time passed and the king grew old, the king wanted to take credit for the prosperity of the kingdom. So he struck down all the statues, all likenesses, and struck Mortinas's name from all official records. Yes, that's it, Mortinas the Elder."

"So he wound up here, in the garbage dump?" Jeff said.

"In the ruins, yes," Harton conceded. "The story says Mortinas was banished from the city. No one knows what ever happened to him, but that was ages ago, and probably just a myth."

"Perhaps," Gennie said thoughtfully.

"Shouldn't you two be returning to the camp area with your loads? All the other children have left. Truit is a cruel task master for those who do not obey his instructions," Harton warned.

"Yes, we should," Gennie said. The two scooped up some remaining bits of stone into their baskets, until they had a full load, but not too much to carry back to the wall.

As they returned toward the great building project along the city's wall, Gennie and Jeff again spoke about the puzzle that still confronted them.

"Jeff, there wouldn't be a statue unless the story was true. That is Mr. Mortimer!" Gennie said.

"I know," Jeff agreed. "It must be a clue to the First Pillar! If we can find out how Mortinas, or Mortimer, brought wealth to the city, that should be the answer."

"We may even be able to find out about all the Three Pillars at once," Gennie added excitedly.

Things were looking up. The heavy load of stone chips seemed light. The day seemed brighter and sunnier. Gone was the dark fear that they would fail and be trapped in this distant place. They were both now firmly convinced that they would be able to solve the riddle of the First Pillar.

CHAPTER 8

The Puzzling Enduro

Encouraged by their discovery, Gennie and Jeff unloaded their baskets of rock fragments at the base of the wall, and quickly slipped away to follow up on their newfound clue. This in itself presented a challenge, as Truit's ever-watchful eye missed little of what occurred in the work area. The two carefully sneaked over to the food tent to ask if anyone knew more about the legend of Mortinas.

Arene, the kind woman who had arranged for Gennie and Jeff to sleep in the tent, was busily making bread. Two other women and the old man Gennie had spoken with the previous

47

night stood idly by, watching the bread making and gossiping about various persons in the encampment.

Arene looked up as Gennie and Jeff approached.

"Are you two done with your work so early?" she asked. "Surely Truit has other tasks for you. I was told you both did a fine job clearing the ramp for the workers."

"Thanks," Gennie said, genuinely proud of the compliment. "We're trying to figure something out and thought you might be able to help us. You won't tell Truit will you?"

At the hint of a secret to be gleaned, the three nosy onlookers immediately stopped their conversation to listen to Arene and the children.

"I won't tell Truit," Arene promised them. "But I will tell you," she added in a quieter voice, "if the truth be told, he has a soft spot for children. He is not nearly so gruff as he pretends. How might I help you?"

"We're trying to find out about Mortinas," Jeff said. "He's the elder who made the city rich."

"A lot of silly nonsense," the old man interrupted. "Talk of the ancient ones is nothing but bedtime stories for children. You will grow up and forget these things."

"Well," Arene interjected, "be they myth or real, it was so very long ago, all the old stories have been forgotten. My grandmother spoke about them, but only in passing."

"It seems funny that no one remembers them," Gennie observed.

"Ah, but there is one person you might ask," one of the gossiping women said, as she anxiously stepped forward, excited to join in the conversation. She was short and round as a melon, with eyes that bulged like a codfish. "You could ask Enduro!"

Upon that, all three of the onlookers burst into laughter.

"Yes, ask Enduro!" volunteered a toothless old woman with a mischievous gleam in her eye. "But be careful you don't catch what ails him, for he is not right in the head!"

The other gossips quickly agreed.

"He is not crazy," Arene said in the man's defense. "He's simply in love. Has it been so long for you three that you cannot remember what that was like?"

"Oh my," the bulging-eyed woman said sarcastically. "Kind Arene has a serpent's tongue."

The other two laughed.

"Be that as it may," Arene said calmly, trying her best to ignore the others, "Enduro would be the one to speak with. His father was a well-known singer of songs, a teller of legends. Enduro may know much about the ancients."

"Beware!" Toothless warned, shaking a bony finger at Gennie and Jeff. "Love alone does not drive a man to do what we have seen Enduro do."

"Not to mention how rude he's been to me," Codfish said.

"A week ago," Toothless continued, "I chanced to pass him. He was drawing circles in the dirt. He would draw circles, scratch a line around them, and then angrily rub them out. He did this again and again and again. It is not a right mind that so delights in some children's game."

"And I have seen him scouring the work area at night," the old man added. "Taking bits of rope and wood and string and twine, like a bird preparing its nest. That is not the work of a sane man."

"It sounds more like the work of a thief," Toothless said.

"Well, he never sleeps!" the woman with the fish eyes added.

"He would have a better chance of winning his girl if he would stop playing with toys. This is something I *do* know about," the toothless old woman said, giving Arene a nasty look. "My nephew accidentally entered Enduro's tent, and inside was a small scaffolding, just like the one Truit has built against the wall. Perhaps inside his tent Enduro pretends he is a giant like Caltor."

The three laughed cruelly.

"Ah, but that's not the worst of it," Codfish said. "My brother says Enduro has sold all his possessions, everything, to pay the metalsmith to make him discs of bronze. Surely those are not the actions of a sound mind."

"Then you haven't heard the latest, have you?" the old man said with an air of superiority.

"What?" the old woman said.

"Tell us, tell us!" Codfish begged. "What have you heard, you sly old dog?"

"Well, yesterday I was walking about on the hillside, and what should I come upon, but Enduro himself, hanging upside down from a tree! A rope was tangled about his leg, the rope thrown high over a branch, and the other end tied to a large rock on the ground," the old man announced.

"Madness!" Toothless concluded.

"Wait until I tell the others about this!" fat Codfish said, nearly drooling with anticipation.

"But," Arene interrupted loudly, "his father *was* a teller of old legends, and Enduro may be able to help you two. His tent is on the edge of camp near a small tree."

Gennie and Jeff thanked Arene, and started out to find Enduro's tent, glad to be rid of the others.

Enduro's tent was tightly closed up. Jeff called out, "Hello, is anybody here?"

"Yes," a voice from inside called out. "Just a moment."

The tent flap quickly jerked aside, and a young man stepped into the bright daylight. He squinted as his eyes adjusted after working inside the darkened tent all morning. As quickly as he had opened the flap, he abruptly closed it behind him, making it impossible to see inside.

"We're looking for Enduro," Gennie told him.

"I am Enduro," he answered. "What is it you want?'"

Enduro's dark features, as well as his gray-white tunic, made the young man look like all the other workers. But the details of his features revealed a driven man. Beneath his brown eyes were large dark half-moons, marking the many nights he had gone with little, if any, rest. The many meals Enduro had missed, being so absorbed in his work, were told in his face's gaunt features. Although only in his mid-20s, he looked ten years older, and already had bits of gray at his temples.

"We were told your father was a poet and singer of songs," Gennie explained. "We're trying to find out about one of the ancient elders called Mortimer."

"Called Mortinas," Jeff corrected.

"Who told you this?" Enduro asked, his eyes glancing about the encampment and work area.

"One of the women in the large tent," Jeff volunteered.

"I see," Enduro grunted.

"Can we come inside, out of the sun, while you tell us?" Gennie asked.

"Yes. Yes, of course. I forgot myself. Please do come in. It's much cooler inside, although quite cluttered," Enduro said.

Enduro pulled back one of the tent flaps and held it open for Gennie and Jeff. It took a few moments for their eyes to adjust to the dark interior. They were astounded by its contents.

A space twelve feet by twelve feet and a little more than six feet high was filled with a jumble of things—great quantities of rope and twine and string, some neatly coiled in orderly piles, and other ropes in a tangled jumble. In the center, a miniature scaffolding, like the one leaning against the great wall outside, stood over small rocks tied to twine.

What appeared to be sheepskins with charcoal-drawn diagrams upon them were scattered about the floor. The diagrams looked like nonsense to Gennie and Jeff. They were pictures of circles, arranged in rows, with lines drawn between and around them. There were perhaps ten drawings, and no two were exactly alike. Some had many circles and some had few. The charcoal line that wove in and out of the circles was different on each of the diagrams, as well. Gennie and Jeff had no idea what the diagrams represented.

In the farthest corner, meticulously arranged upon a sheepskin, were twelve strange bronze discs, each about one foot in diameter. Each of the flat discs had a single hole drilled through its center. Along the outside edge, or circumference of the discs, was a deep groove.

So full was the tent, that there was barely any room for Enduro, let alone for his two small visitors.

"What is all this stuff?" Jeff asked, reaching out to touch the miniature scaffolding. Enduro intercepted Jeff's hand before he could touch the wooden structure.

"Please do not touch anything here," Enduro sternly said to both of them. "You said you had questions about my father. Is that correct?"

"Well, not so much about your father, as one of the ancient elders he might have known about," Gennie explained. "His name was Mortinas."

"Oh yes, you said that. Mortinas, he was the elder of riches," Enduro said thoughtfully.

"Can you tell us about him?" Jeff asked encouragingly.

"I'm afraid that's all I know," Enduro said. "I know who he was, but nothing else. About the time I was old enough to remember my father's stories, he became very ill and entered the world of the dead. I only know a few of his stories, and Mortinas was not in any of them."

"Oh," Gennie said, disappointed. A day that had begun with so much hope, now appeared to come to another dead end in the search for clues to the First Pillar. Jeff gazed down at one of the diagrams closest to his feet.

"What do all these circles mean? Is this some sort of plan for something?" he questioned Enduro.

"That is of no concern of yours! Have you come here to ridicule me like all the others?" Enduro demanded angrily.

"No, we just want information about Mortinas," Gennie answered. Both Gennie and Jeff were somewhat taken aback by Enduro's sudden suspicion.

"I am sorry. I didn't mean to shout at you," Enduro said, wearily rubbing his temples. "For the last two weeks, ever since King Paris commanded the wall to be raised, I have been mocked by many of the workers in the campsite."

"Why? Because of all this stuff? Are you an inventor?" Jeff asked.

"I do not know what an inventor is, but I will tell what these things are for, if you are really interested." Enduro replied.

"Sure!" Jeff said.

"Two weeks ago, King Paris announced that the wall must be raised ten feet because of the advancing Greek fleet," Enduro said.

"Paris promised each group of men one silver stater to share for each stone block pushed to the top of the wall."

"Yes, we heard that yesterday when Hector came to the work area," Gennie reminded him.

"Oh, yes, I forgot. Anyway, for the first few days, I worked day and night to earn as many silver staters as possible. But," Enduro said, extending his arms, "I am not as strong as the other workers. So I had to work long into the night's darkness to earn as much silver as the other workers in the same day. During the time we have left to rebuild the wall, I will never save more than a handful of staters. That will not be enough!"

"Enough for what?" Gennie asked.

Enduro laughed wearily.

"There is a young woman on the other side of the city, Bianda. She is the most beautiful, most wonderful woman I have ever met. We love each other, but by custom we cannot be wed until we have her father's approval. Because I am poor, Bianda's father said he will never give his permission until I have amassed a purse of 50 silver staters!" Enduro sounded exasperated.

"That sounds like an awful lot," Jeff said, "Why don't you just elope?"

"What is elope" Enduro asked.

"Run away and get married. Who cares what her father says!" Gennie said, remembering the countless romance movies she had watched with her mother.

"Bianda has suggested this, but I will not run off and live in shame," Enduro said.

"So what can you do?" Jeff wondered.

"I intend to show her father that I can meet his challenge, no matter how unfair it is," he answered.

54

"What's that got to do with all this stuff?" Jeff said, pointing around the inside of the tent.

"The only way I can earn enough silver is to devise some way to do the work of ten men," Enduro said. "I have been working on this for five days. I have eaten little and only slept a few hours a day, but I feel I am close to the solution."

"What is it?" Jeff asked, dying to know.

"I can only reveal a little to you now. Have you seen how a wheel makes a chariot run swiftly across the ground, so much swifter than if it had none?" Enduro asked.

"Yes," the children answered together.

"Then there must be a way to build a wheel for rope, to make a load seem lighter than it actually is!" Enduro said, his eyes alive with enthusiasm. "When I solve the puzzle, I will share it with you, the camp, the city, and Truit the Taskmaster. Then I shall do the work of a dozen men!"

"Everyone else in the camp thinks you're..." Jeff struggled to find the words that would not hurt Enduro's feelings. He didn't need to worry about Enduro's feelings.

"A fool?" Enduro finished Jeff's sentence.

"Well, sort of," Jeff said sheepishly.

"Do you think I care what others think?" Enduro asked loudly.

"Umm, probably not," Jeff said.

"I will solve this puzzle! Nothing will stop me!" he announced. "I will not just earn 50 silver staters, but 100, or 150! I will show Bianda's father; I will show everyone who doubts me, everyone in the city if need be!"

Enduro's eyes burned with fiery determination. His face had become rigid, his jaw clamped tight. He paced back and forth in the crowded tent. His voice rose so loud that all within a hundred yards could hear of his relentless drive.

"I shall not be defeated by any obstacle! No matter if I do not eat, no matter if I do not sleep, I will solve this equation! I will magnify my strength ten-fold! Nothing will stop me! I will never, never give up!"

Enduro's fury was not directed at Gennie and Jeff, but at the world. After an awkward silence, in which the two were unsure of what to do or say following the outburst, Enduro returned to a more conversational tone.

"You must excuse me. I have had little sleep. But now I must return to my task," Enduro said. "I have solved the first part of the puzzle, and I know I am close to the answer. I am sorry I could not tell you more of Mortinas."

"That's all right," Gennie said.

"I hope you figure it out," Jeff said.

"I shall, young man, I shall," Enduro said.

Gennie and Jeff departed as Enduro returned to his diagrams, the miniature scaffolding, and his bronze rope wheels.

CHAPTER 9

The Rope Wheels

The second day was fast becoming another disappointment for Gennie and Jeff. It seemed no one had heard of Mortinas. What's more, they were still under the watchful eye of Truit the Taskmaster. They spent much of the day sweeping debris from the long wooden ramp to keep the surface clean and smooth.

The work was never ending. After each stone block passed, it left a trail of debris from its slow grinding against the ramp's wooden surface. At any given time, there were as many as ten teams of workers at various points along the ramp, so Gennie and Jeff found themselves running back and forth from stone to stone, continually sweeping and re-sweeping.

◎ Chapter Nine ◎

As the two encountered each team, they relentlessly questioned the workers about Mortinas—did they know of him, could they remember how he brought wealth to the city, did they know anyone who might know of him? But none of the workers knew of Mortinas, let alone the secrets to acquiring wealth. It had all happened too long ago.

High atop the ramp, the two occasionally caught a glimpse of Sarah, the water woman sent here by Mr. Mortimer four years ago. Each time Gennie and Jeff saw her, their hearts missed a beat. She, too, had come back in time at the insistence of a "benevolent" Mr. Mortimer. But now she was trapped. As each minute passed and Gennie and Jeff grew no closer to the First Pillar's secret, they wondered if they would experience the same fate.

After three hours without so much as a short rest, Gennie and Jeff were exhausted. It was hot and tiring work. Truit recognized their weariness and instructed them to come down from the ramp to rest and drink. Truit drove his workers hard, but he had learned the hard way that exhausted workers were the ones most often hurt and injured.

"You are working well," Truit praised them. "I am pleased. For two who seem unaccustomed to hard work, you are doing an excellent job."

"Thank you," Gennie replied wearily.

"Look at your hands now," Truit instructed. Gennie and Jeff looked at their palms, each with numerous blisters from the repetitive sweeping.

"In a few more days, those will turn to calluses. That's the sign of a real worker!" Truit said admiringly.

"I can hardly wait," Jeff said sarcastically.

"I understand you are very curious sweepers as well," Truit said.

"What do you mean?" Gennie wondered aloud.

"I'm told that every man who sets foot upon the ramp is questioned by you about one of the ancients, Mortinas. Is that true?" Truit asked.

"Yes. We're trying to find out how he brought wealth to the city," Gennie explained.

"Have you heard of him?" Jeff asked hopefully.

"In name only," Truit replied. "It is just a myth. Everyone knows wealth is a matter of fate. It is in the hands of the gods. It is best to be content with what you have, than to be unhappy seeking more."

Truit's philosophical outlook about money was like many in camp.

"Have you spoken to Enduro?" Truit suggested. "I believe his father was a singer of ancient songs and stories. He may know of the old legends."

"We spoke to him this morning. He didn't remember anything," Jeff explained.

"He is a peculiar man," Truit said thoughtfully.

"Do you think he's a fool?" Gennie asked, "Everyone else in camp seems to think he's crazy because he's always working on his idea."

"I cannot judge whether he is a fool or not. He has not shared this idea of his with me. I know what others think of him. But I will tell you this," Truit said, leaning closer and lowering his voice so only Gennie and Jeff could hear. "The week in which he worked for me, he was like a demon. He had a fire burning inside of him that never tired, never wavered. His drive was like no man's I've ever seen. I cannot say if this idea you speak of will be successful. But I do know that he has a will of stone, and because of that I would be cautious to judge him too quickly."

As Truit finished his thoughts, he excused himself and returned to supervise the progress of the wall.

As the shadows stretched longer across the work area, Jeff and Gennie grew more concerned. The end of the second day was fast approaching, and they had made little progress in uncovering the mystery of the First Pillar of Wealth. Gennie's suspicion about Caltor had proven correct. He had only taken one stone up the ramp today, and he was not inclined to do anymore. Caltor had wasted their first day.

Now they had spent all this, the second day, trying to learn more about Mr. Mortimer, or Mortinas, as he was known here. But now that, too, looked to be a dead end. No one could remember what he had done, according to the legend, to bring the city riches. How could they solve a puzzle when they didn't have any pieces with which to work? Their hearts were sinking with the setting sun.

"We've tried everybody. No one knows anything about Mortinas," Gennie said, growing more discouraged.

"I think we should go back to Enduro," Jeff suggested.

"Why? He said he didn't know anything, Jeff. That's just wasting time."

"Gennie, when we tried to talk to him, he hardly paid any attention to us at all. He's so wrapped up in whatever he's working on that he didn't even think much about Mortinas, or about his father. I think he just wanted to get rid of us!"

"I suppose so," Gennie admitted. "Maybe if we get him talking about it, he'll mention some sort of clue, something we can figure out. Mr. Mortimer promised us there would be clues and that we could figure it out."

"No, he didn't, Gennie," her brother corrected her. "He *hoped* we were smart enough to figure it out. He never said it was easy."

"All right, we still have one day left," Gennie said, trying to keep a positive attitude. "Let's go ask Enduro again and make sure he really tries to remember. It seems like he ought to know something about it."

They crossed the work area and the large field of tents to Enduro's tent, but before either of them could call to Enduro, one of the tent flaps shot open and Enduro burst out. The three nearly ran into each other.

"You again!" he said, trying to determine what they might want.

"We just want to ask about your father, and Mortinas again," Gennie explained.

"It won't take long. Please?"

Enduro clutched a tightly wrapped bundle under his arm. He looked excited and anxious.

"There's no time for that now! Can I trust you?" he said abruptly, completely changing the nature of the conversation.

"Yes," Gennie said.

"Sure," Jeff agreed.

"Then come with me. Hurry!" Enduro said in a conspiratorial tone. "It's the first half of the equation. I'm going to test it again. Follow me!"

"Can we ask you after you show us?" Jeff demanded.

"What? Yes, oh sure, of course," a distracted Enduro promised.

The three quickly walked to where the wooded hillside began. They pushed their way through the underbrush a short while, until they stopped at a tree, which had a strong low-hanging branch only six feet off the ground.

"You're sure you'll let us ask you about Mortinas?" Gennie asked again.

"Yes. I told you I would help you, didn't I?" he said, as he lay the bundle on the ground and began to unwrap it. "I thought you might like to see this. You both were interested in my diagrams."

Suddenly he froze, and looked at them carefully. "This is a secret you understand; not to be shared with anyone. Do you understand?"

"Yes," the two answered in unison.

Enduro withdrew a long coiled piece of rope and a crudely fashioned, but strong wooden box about the size of a melon from the bundle. Inside the box was one of the bronze discs, held in place by a wooden dowel through the hole in its center. The disc was suspended so it could spin freely. Enduro attached a short piece of rope to the box, and tied it tightly to the tree branch so it hung down like an ornament.

"Now, here is where the magic begins," he said excitedly. He threaded the rope through the bottom of the wooden frame, around the top of the bronze disc, and back out the bottom of the box. He tied a large rock to one end of the rope.

"Now observe!" he proudly said. He pulled on the free end of the rope until it was taut. As he continued to pull, the wheel turned, and the rock was lifted off the ground.

"That's it?" Jeff said.

"Don't you see?" Enduro said. "With my rope wheel, the great stones can be lifted into place rather than dragging them up the ramp! Without the rope wheel, the effort required to lift the stone is too great."

"It's a pulley," Jeff said.

"A what?" Enduro asked.

"A pulley is what we call them," Jeff explained. Enduro wasn't sure he should believe anyone knew of such a thing, or that anyone did.

"You already have these where you come from?" he asked.

"Yes, but I mean, no one has them around here," Jeff back-peddled. He wanted to avoid questions of exactly where he and Gennie were from.

"So with a bunch of men pulling on the rope, the blocks can be raised in a fraction of the time!" Gennie said in a congratulatory fashion.

"Yes, it will be much faster, and I am close to the second part of the puzzle," Enduro said.

"The second part?" Gennie asked.

"I told you this morning that I must raise 50 silver staters," Enduro said.

"We remember," Jeff said.

"This rope wheel alone will not accomplish that. If I cannot solve the rest of the equation, I will gladly show this to Truit for the good of the city. But when twenty or thirty men raise a stone block with my rope wheel, each silver stater will be split very thinly, to twenty or thirty other workers."

"But if it's faster, you'll still earn more," Gennie said, "Because together you'll all be moving so many more blocks."

"True," Enduro conceded. "But the wall nears completion. I must find a way to raise the giant blocks of stone by myself, without any others on the rope!"

"But that's impossible," Jeff said. "You can't lift more than what you weigh. I mean, then the block will pull you off the ground, won't it?"

"Yes, I experienced that yesterday, and was dangling about for some time. It was not pleasant," Enduro confessed, beginning to dismantle the rope wheel from the tree.

"But even if you can't do it alone, because I think Jeff's right, it's still a wonderful invention," Gennie said. "Don't you think you would eventually earn 50 staters?"

"Perhaps, in many years' time. And what of the woman I love? I do not intend to wait a lifetime because her father thinks I'm nothing but a poor fool. While the wall must be raised, there is a brief opportunity, if I can solve the puzzle. And I will solve the puzzle!" Enduro said with fiery determination. "I am close, very close!"

They walked slowly out of the woods back onto the field. The sun had set, and it was beginning to get dark.

"You had questions for me, did you not?" Enduro reminded them, "About my father."

"It's very important for us to find out about the legend of Mortinas, more important than you can know," Gennie said.

"We thought maybe you could try harder to remember," Jeff urged." There must be *something* you remember your father telling you about him."

"You both look very troubled," Enduro observed sympathetically. "I can see this is important to you. This morning after you came to my tent, your questions about the legend made me think of my father. I had not thought of him for many years," Enduro said sadly. "I don't remember a lot about him. I remember some of his legends, wonderful stories of heroes and monsters and great deeds of courage. But he never told me the legend of Mortinas."

Gennie and Jeff could not hide their disappointment.

"I'm truly sorry," Enduro said.

After a few moments of silence, Enduro spoke again. "I do recall my father telling me that one of the ancient elders, whom he never mentioned by name, had been outlawed. My father said he was the greatest of all the ancient ones, but his teachings had been banned by the high priests of the king's court, and were never to be spoken. But my father was careful to never mention his name for fear it might get me in trouble."

They reached Enduro's tent, and he bid Gennie and Jeff goodnight.

"I wish I could help you," he said to them. "Things will look better tomorrow." With that, he disappeared into his tent.

"Tomorrow!" Jeff said to Gennie.

"I know, Jeff," she said, "Tomorrow is the third day!"

It was the middle of the night. Gennie and Jeff were asleep in the large community tent. Outside, the moon was almost full, and lit the large field like a silver beacon. The giant stones from the quarry lay abandoned. Bronze tools and coils of rope were unattended. The stone mason's stands were deserted. The only sounds were the grasses shifting in the gentle wind and rustling in the tents.

As the breeze chanced to lift a flap of the food tent, a sliver of moonlight shone across Gennie's face. For just an instant, as the light swept across her closed eyes, the silver light seemed brighter and more brilliant than anywhere else and a faraway tinkling sound was carried on the breeze. Then it was gone.

Gennie opened her eyes with a start. She sat bolt upright amongst the blankets Arene had given the two.

"Jeff, Jeff. Wake up!" she said in a loud whisper. She shook Jeff roughly by his shoulder until his eyes reluctantly opened and he was more or less awake.

"What? What is it? What's wrong?" he said in a groggy voice.

"I've got it! I've got the answer," Gennie excitedly blurted out. "It's Enduro! He's the one who can lead us to the First Pillar!"

"What about the statue of Mortimer?" Jeff asked, rubbing his eyes.

"That doesn't matter. I mean, not really," she tried to explain.

⑨ Chapter Nine ⑥

"Look, no one remembers anything about that. We spent all day yesterday trying to find something out. But it's like Caltor; it didn't lead us anywhere," she paused to catch her breath.

"But Enduro needs to get 50 silver staters. From what we've seen, that much money would make a person rich, or wealthy."

"If he's able to get it," Jeff added. "He hasn't gotten it yet and may not! What if his idea doesn't work? What if he fails?"

Jeff's question hung heavily in the air for several moments. Neither wanted to say what they were thinking.

"Then we fail," Gennie finally said in a quiet voice.

Failure was a terrifying thought. During the last two days, they'd tried not to dwell on the subject, but now there was no avoiding it. They both knew their deadline was approaching. They knew people really were trapped here. They had come to realize there was no special reason that they should succeed while others, much older than themselves, had failed.

Failure meant never seeing their parents again, for whom they had risked all this in the first place. It meant never seeing their home again, never playing with their friends, never curling up with their two cats. Failure meant a lot of never agains.

"I guess he's the only chance we have," Jeff said thoughtfully.

"He's the only one in the entire camp who's really trying to make money," Gennie said, trying to bolster their confidence. "He's the only one who really, really wants to become rich. Everyone else just talks about it."

"Then tomorrow we better see if there's anything we can do to help him figure out the second part of his idea," Jeff volunteered. "It's our last day, Gennie. You know what that means!"

"I know. But Enduro has to be the answer," Gennie said. "I'm sure of it. I just hope we have enough time."

They laid back down although it was some time before they fell back to sleep. As they listened to the breeze play against the tent walls, they thought about tomorrow, about how they might help Enduro, and about what might happen if time ran out.

CHAPTER 10

The Strength of Ten Men

At the start of the third day, Gennie and Jeff woke early, quickly ate some fruit and bread, and then dashed off to find Enduro. He was their last chance in discovering the First Pillar of Wealth. They arrived at his tent and called out his name, but there was no reply. A woman poked her head out from a tent some thirty feet away.

"If you're looking for the mad man, he left early this morning," she said. "He ran off toward the hillside with a bundle under his arm, laughing and talking to himself."

"Gennie," Jeff said, "Maybe he's solved the puzzle!"

"Let's hope so," Gennie replied.

They walked toward the foothills, to the secluded spot Enduro had led them the previous afternoon.

"Don't blame me if harm comes to you two," the woman called after them. "The man is mad, and I would keep my distance if I were you."

Gennie and Jeff found Enduro right where they expected. He was bent over, unwrapping a large bundle.

"Good morning!" Gennie called to him.

"Did you solve it?" Jeff asked eagerly.

Enduro was smiling. His features looked relaxed and at ease for once.

"Good morning!" he called out. "Remember yesterday I showed you the rope wheel?"

"The pulley?" Jeff countered.

"Yes," Enduro said, with a hint of irritation.

"My rope wheel," he said stubbornly, emphasizing the words *rope wheel*. "The problem has been that if you try to lift a stone heavier than yourself, it pulls you off the ground."

"Yes, that's called gravity," Jeff explained.

"What?" Enduro looked blankly at Jeff.

"Well, in any event, I began experimenting with more rope wheels. And then, late last night while I was observing the moon, I thought, what if a second rope wheel was attached to the stone itself, with the other wheel tied to the tree?"

As he explained his theory, Enduro retied his first rope wheel to the branch of the tree. He threaded the rope through the rope wheel box just as he had done the day before.

"Help me move this stone under the branch," he said, pointing to a rock that was clearly heavier than himself. After several minutes

69

of hard work, the three managed to push and roll the large stone directly underneath the rope wheel. Enduro took a second rope wheel box from his bundle, and a shorter length of rope.

"Here is what had taken me so long to figure out," Enduro confessed. "You see, the stone itself is not actually tied to the long rope you pull on. The long rope simply winds through the second rope wheel."

Gennie and Jeff were a bit lost in trying to follow the explanation.

"Watch, I'll show you," he said. Enduro tied the second rope wheel, or pulley, to the large heavy stone. He took one end of the long rope and threaded it through the top of the second box, down around the bottom of the rope wheel, and back out the top of the box. Finally, he tied the end of the rope to the bottom of the first wheel box, which was hanging from the tree branch.

Gennie was still somewhat puzzled. She repeated the set-up Enduro had explained, following the course of the rope with her hand. "So the rope goes from your hands, around the top of the wheel on the branch, then down around the bottom of the wheel tied to the rock, and then you tie it to..."

"To the base of the first pulley," Jeff finished. "But what's the point? It's impossible to lift more than you weigh!"

"Watch," Enduro smiled.

Enduro pulled on the rope until it was tight. "You agree, then, that this stone is heavier than I?"

"It sure felt like it," Jeff said. "Maybe all three of us could pull it up."

"Or perhaps one," Enduro said, and with that pulled down on the rope. Slowly, the stone rose until it was several feet off the ground.

"But that's impossible!" Jeff blurted out.

"It's amazing," Gennie echoed.

"How did you do it?" Jeff was incredulous. "It doesn't make sense!"

"When I used one rope wheel yesterday, if I pulled down two feet, the rock would rise two feet, would it not?" Enduro asked Gennie and Jeff, as he lowered the rock to the ground.

"Well, yes," Gennie replied.

"Jeff, come here by my side and tell me when I have pulled down two feet of rope. Gennie, you measure how high the stone rises."

The two dutifully got into position as requested. Jeff carefully watched and signaled when it looked as if Enduro had pulled down two feet of the line.

"Stop!" he said, "That's two feet!"

"Gennie," Enduro called out. "How far is the stone off the ground?"

"It only rose one foot," Gennie stammered. "What happened to the other foot?"

"With two rope wheels, when one is tied to the rock, the rope must travel twice as far to lift the stone." Enduro excitedly explained. "But that is what creates the magic! Since I must pull two feet to lift the stone one foot, it has multiplied my strength. Instead of only being able to lift my own body weight, as Jeff mentioned, I can lift..."

"Twice your weight!" Jeff jumped in. "I get it! It's like the gears on my bike that make it easier to ride up hill! I pedal just as fast, but go slower. Gennie, don't you get it?"

"Well, yes, sort of," she answered, still a little unsure of how it worked.

"That's incredible!" Jeff said. "This is really amazing!"

"It is truly wondrous," Enduro agreed, pleased with himself for solving the puzzle. "But think a moment. If I use two rope wheels in this manner to lift twice my weight, could I not use four rope wheels to lift..."

"Four times your weight," Gennie said excitedly. "You're right!"

"Or six," Enduro began.

"To lift six times your weight!" Jeff said.

"If this works," Gennie concluded, "you can lift the big blocks up to the wall all by yourself."

"Yes," Enduro said, smiling. "And I will be able to do it quickly. I could move fifty of the great stones in a matter of days!"

"How many pulleys, or I mean rope wheels, do we need?" Jeff asked.

"*We?*" Enduro asked.

"All we ask is that we can help you in any way possible for the rest of the day," Gennie pleaded. "It's very important for us that you succeed before sunset."

"Before sunset? That is not much time," Enduro said to Gennie, thinking about all they had to do to test the theory on the huge blocks.

"How many rope wheels will we need?" Jeff asked insistently.

"Ten," Enduro replied. "I would rather have too many than too few."

"What do we need to do to get started?" Gennie asked.

"I will draw a diagram of how the wheels must be aligned. Then we must take the drawing, and the bronze discs, to the carpenter," Enduro said. "The weight of the stone blocks are so great, the cabinets that hold the wheels must be very strong. Each of the cabinets will need to hold five wheels."

"We'll take the drawings to the carpenter!" Jeff volunteered.

"Even if he can finish the rope wheel boxes by sunset, that will not leave us any time. To succeed, we need to raise one of the great stones. Only then will Truit and the others understand the importance of my device," Enduro warned.

"We have to try! What else can we do?" Gennie said, unwilling to quit when success was so close at hand.

"Let's get the diagram to the carpenter first," Enduro advised. "You may be able to help him more than I. Let's get back to my tent!"

The three gathered together Enduro's materials and ran back to his tent to prepare the diagrams. For the first time since arriving in this strange place, Gennie and Jeff felt they had a real chance of returning home.

CHAPTER 11

Racing the Sun

The three worked heroically to get everything ready to test Enduro's lifting device before sunset. The carpenter was very demanding, sending Gennie and Jeff on one errand after another. Since the weight of the stones was so great, the wooden cabinets that held the rope wheels had to be reinforced with bronze for support. That took more time. The carpenter had Gennie and Jeff hold the wood as he carefully sawed, measured, and sawed again. When it seemed there was nothing more Gennie and Jeff could do to help, he sent them off to the marketplace to fetch food and drink. The carpenter worked nonstop.

As hard as the carpenter worked the two, they never complained, never slowed their frantic pace, never asked to rest. They were determined and would do anything possible to assist the carpenter in meeting their formidable sunset deadline.

Enduro, for his part, was far from idle. First he had to find a sufficient length of rope. The block had to rise twenty-five or thirty feet. Yet if he had to pull the rope ten feet for every foot of height, the task demanded a rope three hundred feet long! Enduro did not have the money to purchase such a rope. But upon pleading his case to Truit, telling Truit enough to make him curious, but not the full extent of the secret, Truit agreed to help.

"You may borrow the rope for one day only," Truit gruffly agreed. "For I need it back tomorrow!"

The second dilemma to resolve was the scaffolding. It was certainly high enough to attach the top box of rope wheels, rising almost ten feet above the top of the wall. But was it strong enough to support the weight of a stone block? It had been made for the stone masons to walk upon. It looked sturdy enough, but Enduro concluded, there was only one way to find out.

The supply of blocks with which to test the device was the least of their problems. All along the bottom of the scaffolding, lined up for the next few days' work, were twenty-four blocks, resting on the wooden sleds upon which they'd been dragged from the quarry.

Everything was ready and in position. If only the scaffolding would hold, thought Enduro. If only the carpenter can complete the boxes of rope wheels. If only the wheels can support the weight. If only the equation is correct. If only the rope is strong enough. A great many "ifs," Enduro thought. So many things could go wrong in such a short span of time.

In less than an hour, the sun would disappear behind the hills surrounding the walled city. The carpenter had finished, proud of both his handiwork and the short time in which he'd been able to complete the task. The rope wheels themselves, in order to support the large blocks, had been made extremely sturdy. They weighed almost thirty-five pounds each. Gennie and Jeff each carried one of the large pulleys back to Enduro's tent, struggling with the boxes' weight.

"We've got them," Gennie announced. "Look at them!"

She carefully laid the cabinet she'd been carrying down upon a pile of sheepskins.

"It's excellent craftsmanship," Enduro said, closely examining the box of wheels.

Jeff carefully set his down, and Enduro examined that one, as well. "He did a remarkable job in just a day. The frames of the wheel boxes are both wood and metal. That was wise of him. They will need to lift a great deal of weight."

"Can we test them?" Jeff eagerly asked.

"It's almost sundown," Gennie added, once more becoming concerned about their approaching deadline.

"Yes," Enduro said, "The scaffolding looks to be strong enough, and Truit was kind enough to lend us more than enough rope for the task. It is now all up to these," he said, holding out one of the boxes of rope wheels he designed. "Let's go!"

With darkness fast approaching, the workers left the wall area for dinner in the community tent. The work area Enduro had selected was deserted and hidden from the view of the tents.

Enduro first tied one set of the rope wheels to a large block at the base of the scaffolding that hugged the twenty-five-foot wall. Luckily, the sleds the stones rested upon allowed the rope to be passed underneath the blocks. There was no way the three of them could have lifted a stone block by themselves in order to secure the rope. So far, luck seemed to be on their side, but the sun was sinking lower and lower with each passing minute.

Next, Enduro ran up the long ramp with Gennie and Jeff close behind. He needed their help to secure the large, five-wheeled pulley to the top of the scaffolding. The children hoisted it into the air above their heads, while Enduro perched himself atop the wood beams. From there he was able to tie the second box of wheels onto the scaffolding.

Enduro had already dragged the long rope up the ramp and now they had to properly thread the rope in and out of the bronze wheels. First through one wheel atop the scaffolding, then around one wheel down on the stone, then back up to a wheel on the scaffolding and so forth, until all ten wheels had been threaded.

"Jeff and Gennie, go down to the other box of rope wheels and thread the rope through the box as you saw me do it. I'll give you instructions from here," Enduro said.

The two ran down the ramp and positioned themselves by the pulley attached to the stone. As Enduro lowered the end of the rope, Jeff threaded it through the top of the box, down around one of the wheels, and back up through the top of the box. But then he abruptly stopped. Holding the end of the rope, he looked up the twenty-five feet to where Enduro was waiting for the rope to thread through the second wheel. How would he get the rope back up to Enduro?

"Wait a minute!" Gennie said. She found some twine and quickly tied it to the end of the rope Jeff held. Then she tied a small rock to the twine. She threw the rock up to Enduro. He caught it, and pulled the rope to the top of the wall with the twine.

"Good thinking, Gennie," he called to her.

"Not bad, Gennie," Jeff conceded.

The sun was sinking lower. The three completed threading the rope through all ten wheels as the shadows grew longer. The sky glowed dim orange, as it did right before the sun drops from sight.

Enduro completed preparing the device by securing the end of the rope to the bottom of the scaffolding pulley. Finally, everything was ready for testing. Now they had to raise the stone.

"Hurry!" Gennie called to Enduro. "It's almost sundown! We must have the stone raised onto the wall before sunset!"

Enduro raced down the ramp. He didn't understand why the children were so concerned with completing the test before the sun sank, but the tone of their voices convinced him their urgency was serious. Enduro seized the long rope and pulled upon it until it was tight.

"Well, now we'll find out one way or the other," he said.

"Please hurry!" Jeff added, looking into the darkening western sky. "We're almost out of time!"

"All right!" Enduro said. "You two move away from the scaffolding and the stone. If I am wrong in my equation, or the scaffolding beam, or the rope, or the box of wheels itself should give way, I don't want either of you hurt!"

The two obediently moved away from the stone at the base of the wall.

"Okay, we're out of the way, now pull!" Gennie pleaded.

Enduro pulled on the rope. He strained as he pulled in several feet. The scaffolding beams groaned and visibly bowed under the strain. The bronze wheels slowly turned, screeching in revolt as they turned under great pressure upon the bronze shafts within the boxes. And the stone moved!

Enduro struggled to take in more rope, and the large block slowly lifted off the ground a few inches. It started swaying back and forth.

"You two go to the side of the stone and steady it as I lift it farther."

Gennie and Jeff rushed to the heavy stone. On opposite sides, they pushed against the block to steady it. Enduro pulled in several more feet of rope and the large stone rose higher.

"Faster!" Gennie called out.

"You two get back out of the way!" Enduro called out. Again he started pulling in line and raising the stone. The block continued inching upwards. Now four feet above the ground, now six, now ten, now fifteen feet above the ground! There was a large coil of rope about Enduro's feet. His shirt was wet with perspiration. Despite the lifting power of his device, it was still hard work to raise the block.

Jeff saw the coils of rope and ran to remove the clutter from around Enduro's feet. Had the rope slipped from Enduro's hands, and had his feet become entangled in the rope, the plummeting stone would have caused a fatal accident.

"Thank you, Jeff," Enduro said, as he continued to pull upon the rope.

The stone was now almost level with the top of the wall. The rope strained to support the weight. The scaffolding creaked and groaned under the massive block. The bronze wheels continued their screeching, grinding sound. The last few remaining rays of sunlight glimmered above the horizon.

"We're almost there!" Jeff shouted.

"Just a little more," Gennie said happily,

"We're going to make it," Jeff added, "we're going to make it!"

"I just need to rest the stone down on the top of the wall. We will indeed prove this device before sunset," Enduro said through clenched teeth, gripping the rope with all his might.

Then something happened. The rope suddenly went slack.

Enduro fell hard upon his back. The giant stone block tumbled down, crashing to the earth with a mighty thump that shook the ground. Just at that moment, the last remaining rays of light slipped behind the distant hills on the horizon. The sun had set! The test had failed!

"Oh no!" Gennie cried.

"No!" Jeff wailed.

"What happened?" Gennie asked.

"The rope broke," Jeff answered. "And now the sun is gone!"

"The rope did not break," Enduro angrily said, rising to his feet. "It was cut! Look!" He pointed up to the top of the wall.

There, standing like a demon, was Sarah, the water woman. She had a wild look in her eyes and a long knife in her hand.

CHAPTER 12

Second Chance

"It's her!" Jeff said discouraged.

"She's ruined everything!" Gennie said. She was beginning to cry as she realized what their failure meant.

"Did you think I would let you escape from here?" Sarah's raspy voice cut through the still night. "If I cannot leave this rotten place, then you two will not leave it either. Your bones will rot back here in time right along with mine! What do you think of your precious Mr. Mortimer now?"

Gennie and Jeff were stunned. They had lost. Their chance to discover the secrets of wealth, to get home, to help their parents was gone. After being so close, they had lost it all because of this woman's bitterness and her thirst for revenge.

"Do you know this woman?" Enduro angrily asked the two.

"No!" Jeff shouted.

"And what of you?" he asked Gennie.

"No," Gennie quietly answered. She sank to the ground, tears welling up in her eyes.

"Then no one will grieve what I must do!" Enduro said. He picked up a heavy pry bar as if it were a feather. He began walking, slowly and deliberately, up the ramp. His fiery eyes riveted upon Sarah atop the wall.

"After all I have been through. After all I have sacrificed; day after day, night after night, to attain my goal," Enduro said, through his clenched teeth. "And with only a fleeting chance to attain the wealth I need. Do you think I will let you stop me now? Do you think your games will halt my purpose?"

"Stay back," Sarah called out nervously. "I am not afraid of you!" She brandished the knife for him to see.

"All my work will not be destroyed! I will succeed! The stones will rise to the wall! I will obtain the 50 staters, and nothing will stop me!" Enduro shouted.

"I'm warning you," Sarah screamed. "I have a knife!"

Only fifteen feet now separated the two, and for the first time, Sarah could see the expression upon Enduro's face. It terrified her. There was no fear in his eyes, no concern or confusion upon his face. Nothing but a grim determination as if chiseled in stone. He would destroy her if only by the sheer force of his will.

"I warn you," she said in a faltering tone, "I am not defenseless!"

"Nothing will stop me," Enduro growled. "The stones shall rise!"

Enduro took several more steps toward Sarah, who now feared

for her life. As she backed away from Enduro, she lost her footing. With a loud scream, she tumbled backwards, off the wall, and landed outside the city.

Enduro rushed to the edge of the high wall and looked down into the night. He felt satisfaction mixed with concern for the woman's safety. Miraculously, she had landed in tall brush, which had absorbed most of the fall. Enduro could see her below, climbing out of the brush, bruised and shaken, but not seriously hurt. Sarah had fallen outside the walled city. After that time, no one recalls ever seeing the water woman again.

Enduro walked back down the ramp to the ground to carefully examine the stone that had fallen from atop the wall.

"We are in luck!" he called to Gennie and Jeff. "The box of rope wheels was not damaged in the fall. We can try again to raise the stone!"

"It doesn't matter anymore," Gennie said sadly.

"We'll never get home," Jeff whimpered.

"What do you mean?" Enduro said, walking over to where the two sat.

"We're not from here," Gennie said, wiping tears from her eyes. "Mr. Mortimer, or Mortinas, sent us here to discover the first secret to wealth. But we only had three days. If we didn't find it by then, we wouldn't be able to go home. You were our last hope, and now the day is over."

"So that explains all the questions about my father and about Mortinas," Enduro said thoughtfully. "When did you first arrive here?"

"Three days ago," Jeff snapped.

"But what time of the day?" Enduro asked.

"What time?" Jeff said, a bit confused now.

"Time of the day?" Gennie repeated.

"Yes," Enduro said. "What time of the day?"

"Uh, morning, later in the morning," Gennie said, beginning to brighten.

"Everyone had already eaten breakfast," Jeff said, looking up hopefully.

"Don't you see?" Enduro said." It won't be three full days until tomorrow morning. There is still time!"

Gennie's and Jeff's tears stopped as if turned off by a switch. Jeff quickly ran through the three days upon his fingers. Gennie did the same figuring in her head. They turned to each other simultaneously and said in unison, "He's right!"

"We still have time!" Jeff said half-laughing and half-crying.

"Yes. Thankfully it would appear you still have time," Enduro smiled.

"Then we must get to work immediately!" Gennie announced.

"You don't want to rest?" Enduro said, teasing both of them.

"No!" Jeff said, jumping to his feet.

"We're too close to stop now!" Gennie said. "We can work through the night if we have to."

"We will work all night! I'm not even tired!" Jeff added.

"Then work we shall," Enduro said smiling. "The moon will give us ample light. One more sleepless night will not matter now. Let us perform such a feat that the entire city will never forget!"

The children wiped off their tear-stained faces and, with a determination they'd never felt before, began their long night's work.

CHAPTER 13

The First Pillar
Is Revealed

It was several hours before sunrise when the three finally stopped working. They were so exhausted that it would have been foolish to continue. Enduro had not had a full night's sleep in weeks. Gennie and Jeff, having worked tirelessly through the night, combined with the stress of the previous three days, were spent. They returned to Enduro's tent for some well-earned rest. As each lay down in their respective corners of the tent, they fell asleep the moment their heads touched the soft sheepskin.

The first light of dawn reached across the field of tents and awoke Truit. As usual, Truit

85

was the first to rise. He dressed quickly and slowly paced through the field, while all around him were just stirring. Truit often did this to plan the workers' activities for the coming day. As he approached the work area, he chanced to look up at the top of the wall along the scaffolding.

"Great heavens!" he gasped, falling to his knees.

Three hours after sunrise, Enduro slowly awoke. There seemed to be a great deal of noise outside. It sounded like the subdued voices of many people.

"Enduro!" a loud voice called out. Enduro jumped up just as a soldier boldly entered the tent.

"Are you Enduro?" the soldier asked.

"Yes," a puzzled Enduro replied.

"Your presence is required at the work site," the soldier commanded. "Please come with me now!"

"All right," Enduro answered. "Just let me get my things together." Enduro gently nudged the two children with his foot. "Gennie, Jeff, wake up! Something is wrong!"

"What is it?" Gennie asked sleepily.

"Something has gone wrong at the wall," Enduro said. He was becoming seriously concerned. "I must go."

"We'll come with you," Jeff said, rubbing the sleep from his eyes.

When the soldier and the three emerged, they found almost everyone in the entire campsite gathered around Enduro's modest tent. The moment Enduro stepped into the open, the camp erupted in loud cheers and applause.

"What is all this?" Enduro asked.

"It must be your lifting device," Gennie said, yelling to be heard above the cheers of the crowd.

"Is this all for me?" Enduro asked in disbelief.

The soldier turned to face Enduro. "It is all for you. And you have the army's thanks as well, Enduro! But we must hurry. Hector has summoned you to the work site."

"Hector!" Enduro repeated.

Enduro pushed his way through a sea of smiling, cheering faces. Everyone in camp wanted to congratulate Enduro, to thank him, to laugh with him, to be a part of his success. Enduro's weary expression gradually changed to one of happiness and joy. For the first time in weeks, he permitted a broad smile to cross his face.

Hands reached out to pat him on the back and shoulders, or to shake his hand in appreciation. Suddenly a huge paw of a hand reached through the crowd. Enduro looked up to see Caltor smiling down at him. Caltor took Enduro's hand and shook it hard.

"Well done," the giant said. "Well done!"

The crowd of well-wishers followed Enduro to the work area. There Enduro found a small group of workers and nearly a dozen soldiers. In the center stood Hector, speaking to Truit. The soldier escorted Enduro, Jeff, and Gennie to the famous commander of the city's armies.

"So this is the wise Enduro," Hector said.

"Hector, it is a great honor!" Enduro said.

"No, Enduro, the honor is mine," Hector said genuinely, reaching out to shake Enduro's hand. "For what you have created may well save our city."

Hector looked behind him to the top of the wall. There, perched high atop the structure, were twelve huge stone blocks neatly lined up, awaiting the stone masons. The blocks proclaimed to the entire camp the wonder of Enduro's rope wheels. One man and two children had accomplished the work of a dozen men, and in much less time!

"I awoke this morning at first light," Truit explained to Hector. "And when I saw the stone blocks upon the wall, that were not there the night before, I thought here was the work of the gods. And then I saw the rope I had given Enduro last night."

"I forgot to bring the box of rope wheels," Enduro suddenly remembered, much to his alarm. "Where are they?"

"King Paris is examining them," Hector explained.

"The king?" Enduro stammered. "The king himself?"

"It is a remarkable device. With more of them, we can raise the walls in a matter of weeks instead of months," Hector said.

"As I had wished," Enduro said. He looked around at the large crowd and the many soldiers, a bit embarrassed. "You accomplished much while I was sleeping this morning."

"It is you who accomplished so much," Hector said.

"It was all of us in this camp who were asleep for the last two weeks while you created your lifting device," Truit added.

Hector raised his voice so that all gathered could hear him. "When King Paris was told of this remarkable device this morning, he instructed us to bring it to him. Upon examining it, we believe that with many more of Enduro's remarkable devices, we will be able to raise the walls well before the Greek fleet lands upon our shores!"

The crowd cheered. Hector laid a hand upon Enduro's shoulder. "And King Paris has bestowed upon Enduro, for creating his lifting device and single-handily helping to fortify the city, a prize of 100 silver staters!"

The entire encampment cheered. Enduro turned to Gennie and Jeff.

"Thank you for your help. I could not have done so much without your assistance." Just as Gennie and Jeff exchanged a high five, the two became surrounded in a great column of swirling mist and starlight. Moments later, to the astonishment of the crowd, Gennie and Jeff were gone.

The shimmering stars swirled around Gennie and Jeff faster and faster, becoming a blur of brilliant colors. The swirling gradually slowed, and disappeared altogether.

The two found themselves back in the great temple hall, standing before the three massive Pillars of Wealth. Near the pillars was a smiling Mr. Mortimer, his familiar face a welcome sight for Jeff and Gennie. The two children ran to the ancient man's side.

"We made it!" Gennie said excitedly. Her happy voice echoed about the huge chamber.

"You were indeed successful," Mr. Mortimer said.

"We found an old statue of you, Mr. Mortinas, I mean Mr. Mortimer," Jeff said, correcting himself.

"Ah, the statue in the ruins. I remember. That was a very long time ago," he said, reflecting for a moment on the past.

"What happened to Enduro?" Gennie asked.

"He married the woman he loved," Mortimer said contentedly.

"And what about the war?" Jeff asked.

"That is of no concern," Mortimer replied.

"But what happened to the city inside the wall?" Jeff asked insistently.

"Well," Mr. Mortimer said, carefully choosing his words. "The walls were never breached. Now, tell me. What did you learn during the last three days?"

"Well, we thought Caltor would earn lots of money, so we followed him around the first day," Gennie began.

"But it turned out he never worked very hard," Jeff added. "He really just wanted to talk about money. Then we met Enduro..."

"He needed to earn 50 silver staters, so he worked all the time and invented a pulley thing so he could lift the blocks and earn the money," Gennie explained.

"Yes, he never stopped trying," Jeff finished.

"Then you two have discovered for yourself the First Pillar of Wealth," Mr. Mortimer said. "Go to the base of the great column and look once more."

Gennie and Jeff rushed to the massive pillar that rose into the darkness. They quickly surveyed its base. On the bottom portion, cut deep into the marble a foot high were the letters D-E-S-I-R-E.

"It says 'desire'," Gennie announced.

"Desire?" Jeff repeated. Mr. Mortimer joined the children at the base of the pillar.

"From the First Pillar, all else flows," Mr. Mortimer said, quoting himself. "Do you remember my saying that?"

"Yes," Jeff answered, "before we left."

"Without the desire for wealth, it will never occur," the old man explained. "Enduro had within him a burning desire that could not be extinguished. He wanted to succeed more than anyone else in the camp. So fierce, so committed, so steadfast was he, that nothing could have stopped him from earning the 50 staters. Tell me, Gennie, did you ever think he would quit?"

"No," Gennie answered, "he was so intense."

"Jeff, did you ever think he would not accomplish his goal, or that some obstacle might stop him?" Mr. Mortimer asked.

"Well, I guess we weren't sure, but he never doubted himself, not once," Jeff replied thoughtfully.

"Then you have learned the first lesson well. Without the true desire to attain wealth, nothing else will follow. The laborer will not work hard enough, long enough," Mortimer paused to emphasize his last point, "or work *smart* enough. Without a desire burning from within, the dreams of wealth are nothing more than fantasy."

"That's what Caltor did," Gennie observed.

"Exactly! A true burning desire for wealth tempers one for the task. From the desire for wealth, all else will flow."

"But doesn't everyone want to be rich?" Jeff asked.

"Of course, Jeff, everyone wants to be rich," the old man repeated, "but most fall by the wayside just as Caltor did. Caltor dreamed of easy riches but was unwilling to work to attain them, even though his great strength put riches well within his reach. There is a great difference between simply wanting wealth, and steadfastly setting a course to acquire it. Enduro had it. Why, that spark was even within both of you."

"What do you mean?" Gennie asked.

"Think about the last night of your visit," Mortimer asked them.

"We worked all night," Jeff said proudly.

"Yes! That night the fire was inside of you!" Mortimer said. "Were you not determined to raise the blocks atop the wall?"

"Yes," Gennie replied.

"Would you have let anything stop you?" he asked Jeff.

"No, I guess not," Jeff said.

"It's that same determination, that same drive, that same desire which forms the First Pillar of Wealth," Mr. Mortimer concluded.

"Are all the pillars so…hard?" Gennie sheepishly asked, already worried about what Mr. Mortimer might have in store for them on their next journey.

"No," he smiled warmly. "The First Pillar is the most difficult because it is the most important. If the desire is missing, the other two pillars collapse into sand. They would be meaningless. I am proud of how well you two did, very proud. From now on, trust in yourselves. The secret of the pillars will always be close at hand."

Mr. Mortimer handed Gennie a papyrus scroll bound with a red seal of wax.

"The Second Pillar awaits. Seek out the household of Augustus Diocus. This note will explain that you are distant cousins from the province of Gaul, awaiting the arrival of your parents in three days."

He handed Jeff a small leather pouch of coins.

"This money will ensure that they welcome you as family. The Second Pillar will be revealed within the walls of their house. You may return after midnight on the third day." He paused for a moment. "If you are successful."

Once more Gennie and Jeff were surrounded in the silver-like mist and a shower of dazzling starlight. A moment later, they were gone from the huge chamber.

THE SECOND PILLAR

CHAPTER 14

Ancient Rome

They stood in a large square, with a bright sun overhead in a cloudless blue sky. Ornate temples of white stone supported by huge Corinthian columns—similar to the even larger pillars Mr. Mortimer had presented—stood all around them. The columns adorned all the buildings surrounding the square, but it was the countless statues that made the square so remarkable.

Statues of various gods and goddesses perched atop the buildings high overhead. Three muses played musical instruments on one temple. Four stone horses pulling a chariot, whose driver held the wreath of victory skyward, a tribute to both emperors and champions, topped a large archway in the square's center. Across the square was a large building decorated with twelve archways on each of its four stories. Within each archway, stood a ten-foot-tall statue. On top of this building, additional statues were spaced every twenty feet. Throughout the square, on obelisk-like columns of highly polished marble, stood a winged woman with outstretched arms—the statue of victory.

The overall effect was stunning. For many minutes, Gennie and Jeff simply gazed in wonder, spellbound by the grandeur.

More than one hundred people occupied the square, but they weren't crowded. The people were engaged in conversations and strolled more leisurely than Gennie and Jeff witnessed back home. Most of the men and women were dressed in white togas, covered with white cloaks made of linen, which were loosely wrapped about their bodies.

Gennie and Jeff realized they were dressed similarly, although their togas and cloaks appeared to be a little more worn and tattered. The sandals on their feet looked considerably nicer than the footwear they wore on their last quest.

After asking several people for directions, they wound their way through a maze of narrow roadways in search of Augustus Diocus's house, an endeavor made more difficult due to the lack of street names. They also had to dodge the occasional chariot, small carts pulled by donkeys, and rich citizens who reclined atop litters carried by servants or slaves. Most of the people on the roadways, however, traveled by foot. At last they found the building. It seemed large for a house, and was quite dreary on the outside. It had no windows overlooking the narrow roadway. They walked up to the porch area, unsure of what to expect.

Gennie knocked on the large wooden door. A man wearing a

white toga and cloak opened it. "Yes, whom do you seek?" he asked them.

"We're looking for Augustus Diocus's family," Gennie said. "We were told this is his house."

"I am Augustus Diocus. What is it you want?"

Augustus Diocus looked to be about forty, with blond hair turning to gray. He was taller than most of the people Gennie and Jeff had seen that morning. His toga and the many folds of his cloak could not hide his ample belly. A corpulent red face indicated he was accustomed to large quantities of rich foods.

"We're your cousins, from Gaul!" Gennie said. She handed Augustus the scroll that Mr. Mortimer assured them would gain them entry into the household. Augustus unrolled it and began to read. A woman walked to his side.

"Do we have guests, Augustus dear?" she asked. This was Dovenia, Augustus's wife. She looked quite small standing next to Augustus. Her small features and light brown hair gave her a mouse-like appearance.

"It seems so," Augustus said, still reading the scroll. "It would seem I have a cousin Mortenius in Gaul. A distant cousin to be sure, at least not one that I was aware of. He and his wife will be arriving in Rome in three days."

"Did you hear that Gennie?" Jeff whispered. "We're in Rome!"

"He asks us to care for these two, his children, until he arrives, Augustus continued. "Their names are Gennie and Jeff."

"Yes, I'm Jeff."

"And I'm Gennie."

"What curious names," Augustus said. "But then we hear many things are quite different in the provinces."

"This is a difficult time for guests," Dovenia said in a loud whisper to her husband. "We have the celebration and feast to pre-pare for. I am not sure we have room for them."

"Yes," Augustus thought aloud. "We certainly don't need two more mouths to feed at this time. Yet, they are still family, no matter how far removed."

"Are we to take strangers into our home based upon the ink on this scroll?" Dovenia whispered.

Jeff stepped forward and held out the leather pouch of coins. "I was told to give you this, to pay you for letting us stay here for the three days." He handed the pouch to Augustus, and it was quickly opened. Augustus's eyes gleamed as he looked at its contents.

"By the gods," he exclaimed. "There must be 100 denarii here! Now that I think of it, I am sure I recall a cousin Mortenius. Yes, I am quite sure. In Gaul you say?"

"Yes," Gennie said.

"Certainly!" Augustus said, quickly closing the pouch and putting it within the many folds of his cloak. "You are more than welcome! Please come inside and meet my family."

Gennie and Jeff entered, and the large wooden door closed behind them.

The inside of the house was a remarkable contrast to the dreary outside. In the center of the large, one-story home was an atrium containing a small courtyard, perhaps thirty feet across, which was open to the sky. In each corner of the square-shaped courtyard were white marble statues of gods. In the center, a small fountain gurgled water from the mouths of mythical beasts. The courtyard itself was ringed with flowers and exotic plants. All the rooms were positioned on the outside of the atrium, like spokes radiating from the center of a wheel.

The opulence of the house was breathtaking. Colorful mosaics of intricate design covered the floors. Columns in the entryway and throughout the house were of white, green, and pink marble, polished to a high gloss. Walls throughout the house were painted with vibrant colors, depicting scenes of daily life. Oil lamps on stands lit the perimeter of the entryway.

Augustus called two older children standing near the entry hall.

"Marcus, Androne! Come meet your cousins from Gaul!"

The two reluctantly walked over.

"This is Gennie and Jeff," Augustus said. "They will be staying with us for several days until their parents arrive from Gaul. They are distant cousins. I'm sure the four of you will have many things in common."

"Hi!" Gennie and Jeff said. They both thought this visit wouldn't be so bad with some other kids in the house. But that turned out to be very wrong.

Marcus, Augustus's sixteen-year-old son, was several inches taller than Gennie. He mirrored his father's tall and light features, only he was much fatter, with almost a *doughy* look to him.

Androne, the daughter, was thirteen just like Gennie. She was a pretty girl with brown eyes and bright auburn hair, worn in a wraparound style that hid her ears. Her toga was immaculate. Like her brother, she was terribly conceited.

"My god, look at their clothes!" Androne said.

"Have they no tailors in the provinces?" Marcus asked arrogantly.

"Where are they going to sleep?" Androne asked. "Not in my room!"

"Please!" Augustus cut them off. "They are family, and you will treat them as such!"

"I'm sorry," Dovenia said to Gennie and Jeff, remembering her manners. "We are all a little frantic with the events of tonight. You are welcome in our house. We have a storeroom with several extra beds in it that you can use."

"And I imagine this is your first trip to Rome," Augustus said. "Perhaps we'll be able to show you some of the sights tomorrow. You will find many things different here in Rome, but I'm sure you'll find them wonderful!"

"You can wait in the courtyard while our servants prepare your room," Dovenia said, gesturing toward the atrium.

"Thanks," Jeff said.

Gennie and Jeff walked through the luxurious entryway toward the courtyard to await Dovenia's instructions.

CHAPTER 15

The Secret to Augustus's Wealth

Augustus warmly greeted a small man dressed in plain brown robes who arrived at the house. The two walked through the atrium toward the room that served as an office for Augustus.

"Excuse me," Gennie interrupted as they discussed business. "Do you have a few moments to explain something to Jeff and me?"

"Well, I have business to conduct, but if it's quick." Augustus answered.

"My father says you're very wise about money," Gennie said, trying to flatter Augustus. "He said if I ever want to know anything about becoming rich, I should talk to you."

Augustus laughed heartily.

"You hear that, Tirocles? Even in the provinces they know of my shrewd business sense."

"It would appear so," the smaller man replied.

"Tirocles, these are the children of my third cousin, from the northern provinces of Gaul," Augustus said. "This is Gennie and Jeff. This is Tirocles. He is my clerk. We both work at Tacitus's Trading House. Let's all go into my office and I can answer your questions."

As they walked across the atrium to Augustus's office, Augustus leaned over and whispered to Tirocles. "Their parents are third or fourth cousins I've never met. I think they are simply taking advantage of my hospitality."

With the office door closed behind them, Augustus sat his ample frame in a chair behind a small desk. The desk had several papyrus scrolls, an inkstand, and four or five pens upon it. Gennie and Jeff sat in wooden chairs, while Tirocles, the clerk, stood.

"So, you two want to know how I have become so rich, is that it?" Augustus asked.

"Yes," Jeff answered. "We understand you've uncovered a secret to wealth."

"Well, I don't think it's a secret. It's just been a matter of hard work. Both Tirocles and I have worked for Gracchus for nearly twenty years. Isn't that right, Tirocles?" Augustus asked his clerk for confirmation.

"Eighteen years to be exact," Tirocles corrected.

"Our employer, Gracchus Tacitus, started in business by trading secondhand clothes as a boy," Augustus explained. "He then started trading in oil. He bought small amounts from the ships in the wharf, and took them by cart up into the city where he could sell the oil to housewives who preferred not to make the journey. He eventually built that small business into a trading company with three ships. Today we trade with the farthest corners of the earth— Persia, Syria, Mesopotamia, Tyre, Sidon, Phoenicia, Egypt, and Judea.

"But Gracchus's real *secret,* and one I have dutifully copied, is hard work," Augustus said proudly. "I toil longer than any of my neighbors. I often leave for work before dawn and return from work after sunset."

"You are indeed a hard worker," Tirocles added.

"You have the *desire* to be wealthy," Gennie observed.

"Yes, that is well said," he complimented Gennie. "And because I have worked long and hard, I have been able to acquire the riches you see around you."

"Anything else?" Jeff asked.

"Isn't that enough?" Augustus laughed. He looked thoughtful for a moment. "Tirocles," he said, handing the clerk a papyrus scroll, "here are the market estimates for our three ships due from Alexandria. Gracchus wishes you to compare these numbers against our costs to estimate our profits."

"All right," Tirocles replied. "I can complete these this afternoon."

"Good. That is all for today," Augustus said, dismissing his clerk.

"Thank you. Enjoy your banquet tonight," Tirocles said. "I understand Gracchus himself will be attending."

"Yes," Augustus said, a bit embarrassed Tirocles knew of the banquet. "I would have invited you but my son…"

"Say no more. I understand," Tirocles said, and left the room, closing the door behind him.

Augustus waited in silence for several moments after Tirocles left.

"As relatives, I thought I might share something else with you, something I don't think it necessary for Tirocles to hear."

"He works for you?" Gennie asked.

"Well, yes," Augustus answered. "Actually it was I who suggested that Gracchus hire him. I'd been with the company about a year and Tirocles and I had been friends, so when Gracchus said he needed yet another clerk, I suggested it be Tirocles. Tirocles had been down on his luck and needed a job very badly. We worked side-by-side for fifteen years. Then three years ago Gracchus promoted me above Tirocles. As a result, my income has increased substantially!"

"Because you're a harder worker than Tirocles?" Jeff asked.

"Well, Tirocles is also a very hard worker," Augustus admitted.

"So all your wealth is because you've been making more money these last three years?" Gennie asked, wanting to be absolutely clear.

"Partly," Augustus leaned forward and spoke in a hushed tone. "But most of the luxuries you see before you, including tonight's banquet, are the result of a secret I have discovered."

"What is it?" Gennie asked eagerly. It was beginning to sound like they would discover the Second Pillar of Wealth in no time at all.

"Debt," Augustus whispered.

"Debt?" Jeff repeated.

"Yes! If I had to pay for all these wonderful things all at one time, I could not afford them," Augustus confided to the children. "But by borrowing from money lenders, I can obtain a great deal of money now, and pay the money lenders in smaller amounts over time."

"So all this is bought with borrowed money?" Jeff asked, gesturing around the richly appointed room.

"Not *all* of it, but most of it," Augustus admitted. "Now I must confess, the small payments I must make have become quite large, totaling most of my salary. However, so long as I can make those payments, I'm able to enjoy a lifestyle much higher than others in my position."

"That sounds good, I guess," Jeff said, ever so slightly unsure.

"And, of course, I've borrowed even more lately since I know we will have a huge profit from our recent trading with Alexandria," Augustus said proudly. "In fact, that's how I have paid for the lavish banquet tonight. I have borrowed against the money we will earn when we sell the goods from Alexandria."

"I see," Gennie said thoughtfully. Augustus leaned back in his chair.

"Your father was correct, was he not?" Augustus boasted.

"Well, I guess so," Gennie tentatively replied.

"Much can be accomplished with a shrewd mind," Augustus smiled. "Now then, there is still much to be done for Marcus's banquet. We can talk more of this if you wish at a later time."

Augustus rose to his feet and walked to the door with Gennie and Jeff close behind.

"Thank you," Gennie said. "You've been a big help."

"My pleasure," Augustus said, as they walked across the atrium. Androne, his pampered daughter, met Augustus. "There you are," he said to Androne. "Where have you been?"

"I was trying on my gown for tonight! It's beautiful!" Androne exclaimed. "Thank you so much, Father!"

"I'm glad. You should talk with your cousin Gennie," Augustus told his daughter. "She has a remarkable head for business, very rare in a young woman. A very smart child indeed!"

"Really. How wonderful," Androne said sarcastically. "We shall have to do something about that," she added under her breath.

Gennie and Jeff excused themselves from Augustus and his daughter to return to the small room they would be using for the next few days.

The room was a large storeroom filled with dust-covered furniture, including two small beds.

"Do you think he's right," Jeff asked Gennie, "about borrowing money being the Second Pillar?"

"I don't know. He has gotten a lot of stuff by doing it," Gennie said. "They have this great house and servants! And he has the First Pillar—desire!"

"Yes, but borrowing money is something Mom and Dad always argue about. Like they really yell about it," Jeff said sadly.

"I know. It also seems like this was way too easy for us," Gennie observed. "Mr. Mortimer warned us it would be really hard to discover the pillars. I mean, we've only been here a little while!"

"Let's keep looking," Jeff concluded. "We have three days to find out. If the Second Pillar is debt, or borrowing, maybe there's some special trick about how to do it."

CHAPTER 16

The Spider's Web

Androne stood in the doorway of her mother's and father's bedroom.

"Mother, might I have a word with you?" Androne asked politely.

"Why certainly," Dovenia said. "Come in."

Dovenia was preparing her gown and her husband's toga for the evening's banquet. Androne picked up a small hand mirror of her mother's and fussed with her large curls while gazing at her image.

"Mother, it is such a shame that dear Gennie cannot join us at the banquet," Androne said, putting the mirror back down.

"That is kind of you to say, Androne. But we have no room for her," Dovenia told Androne what she actually already knew. "With your brother's friends, the few neighbors, and Gracchus Tacitus and his wife, whom your father invited."

"Oh, why does that stuffy old man have to come?" Androne asked, irritated.

"You know very well," Dovenia corrected Androne. "He owns the trading house where your father works. It is wise to gain the favor of your superiors."

"Yes, I suppose so," Androne said, picking up a floating flower from a decorative water-filled bowl. She spun it coyly between her fingers. "Well, as I said, poor Gennie will not be able to dine with us tonight."

"I'm sure Marcus's friends would have liked another young lady at the banquet," her mother observed.

"Yes..." Androne said darkly.

"I think there will be ample food left over," Dovenia said. "Gennie and Jeff will be able to sample cuisine the likes of which they have never known."

"Yes, but it is such a shame Gennie cannot actually see the banquet, to observe Roman society," Androne said. "She may never get a chance again, and I'm sure it would mean a great deal to her."

"Well, that is probably true," her mother said, a bit unsure what Androne was getting at.

"I was thinking that if perhaps she helped at the banquet, then she could observe proper society," Androne purred.

"That is a wonderful idea!" Dovenia agreed. "She can help Secunda serve. I'm sure she wouldn't mind. She certainly ought to help out. And in that way she can see a true Roman banquet."

"Yes, that would be nice," Androne said, her voice sweet as honey but her eyes narrow as a poisonous snake's. "But father has spent so much on the exotic dishes, and the banquet is so important to Marcus, I would hate to see Gennie's nervousness, or perhaps even clumsiness, spoil the banquet. I mean, you know how some of these provincial girls are. It would ruin everything, and what with Gracchus here, too."

"Yes, that would be terrible," her mother agreed thoughtfully. "What shall we do?"

"Perhaps she could wash the hands and feet of our guests," Androne slyly suggested.

"Androne, that is the lowliest of tasks. I have even dreaded asking Secunda," Dovenia said. "Gennie is a guest in our house and a relative, even though a distant one."

"Oh, I know, Mother. But it would break my heart if we could not enrich her about Roman society. I feel I owe it to my dear cousin. Yet to serve the main food, well, it would be such a shame if something happened," Androne said cunningly.

"Very well. Perhaps it would be good for the child," Dovenia gave in. "I'm sure she is used to such things."

"Oh, I'm sure she'll be very pleased, Mother. Very pleased. I will tell her the good news myself," Androne said.

"I have to what!" Gennie exclaimed. Gennie and Jeff had been talking in their room when Androne informed them of their plans for Gennie.

"I tried to talk her out of it, but my mother is so headstrong she just would not be swayed," Androne said. "I begged her to let one of the servants perform the task. After all, it is so, so plebeian."

"I have to wash everyone's feet?" Gennie stammered.

"Yes, and their hands. Mine, too!" Androne couldn't help but smile. "And the hands are to be washed between each course."

"And you tried to talk your mother out of it?" Gennie asked, beginning to see through Androne's little game.

"Oh, indeed, dear cousin," Androne said, dripping with sweetness. "And, Gennie, please talk to Secunda, our household servant. Do try and find something more appropriate to wear tonight."

Gennie looked down at the plain tunic she was wearing. Androne casually turned and walked out of the room into the atrium.

CHAPTER 17

Preparing for the Feast

The breathtakingly beautiful dining room was framed with gentle ceiling arches that reached a height of ten feet and were painted red and gold. The four walls, painted in great detail, depicted peaceful garden and woodland scenes. All around were arrangements of exotic and fragrant flowers. Even the floor, thirty feet by thirty feet, was a work of art. It was an intricate mosaic, made with thousands of small, colorful tiles. Pictured on the floor were the Roman household gods Vesta, of the hearth fire; Lares, who guarded the home; and Pentates, spirit of the larder. It was like dining in a mystical garden of the gods.

Nine ornate couches for banquet guests to recline upon to dine were placed around the room. They were made of rich inlaid mahogany with gold-leaf trim. Each couch had a small matching footstool before it.

Dovenia led Gennie and Jeff to the far end of the room where a pretty, but plainly dressed woman was making the finishing touches on one of the large floral arrangements.

"Secunda," Dovenia announced. "This is Jeff and Gennie. They are distant cousins of Augustus from Gaul. They will be staying with us for a few days. They can help you with the banquet tonight."

"Very good," Secunda replied obediently.

"Gennie will attend to the sandals and washing of our guests," Dovenia said. "And see if you can find something to keep young Jeff busy in the kitchen."

"But surely you do not wish for a guest of yours and a cousin of Augustus to attend to the feet and hands of Marcus's friends? If there is no one else, I will perform the task," Secunda volunteered.

"No, Secunda. The food alone will require your full attention. I'm sure Gennie does not mind. Augustus and Marcus are leaving for the forum," Dovenia continued, "we must be ready this evening for their return."

Dovenia abruptly left the room.

"I'm pleased to meet you," Secunda said politely. "My name is Aphrodite Secunda. I am the cook and one of the household servants for Augustus."

"Should we call you Aphrodite or Secunda?" Gennie asked.

Secunda frowned. "Within these walls, it would be best if you called me Secunda. Upon my birth, my proud father thought I was the most beautiful of baby girls, as all fathers do," she said to Gennie. Gennie smiled in understanding.

"So he named me Aphrodite the second, or Secunda, after the goddess. It is a silly name," she admitted. "But young Androne didn't want another in the household to be called Aphrodite, so she insisted that I just be called second. I think it amuses her a great deal. Hence, within these walls, I am Secunda."

"We already know about Androne," Jeff said. "She's a major pain!"

"Duh! That's an understatement!" Gennie added.

"Hopefully, she will outgrow her...," Secunda paused to select her words carefully, "high spirits. In any event, your visit is at an excellent time. The household has been preparing for many months for Marcus's Feast of Liberation."

"What's that?" Gennie asked.

"Several days ago, Marcus turned sixteen. I don't know of your customs in Gaul, but in Roman society, the sixteenth birthday is when a boy passes into manhood," Secunda explained. "This afternoon, Marcus and Augustus, his father, and several of Marcus's close friends will go to the forum for a special ceremony."

Secunda looked at Gennie. "The women of the household are not permitted to attend."

"That's not fair!" Gennie complained.

"It is the way it has always been," Secunda explained.

"That doesn't make it right," Gennie stubbornly replied.

"In the ceremony, Marcus will exchange the toga he now wears, the toga of childhood with the red border, for the plain white toga of manhood. This afternoon he will also receive his first shave."

"No wonder he looked so scruffy this morning," Gennie said. "He should have had his first shave a long time ago!"

111

"Well, yes," Secunda laughed. "I think many of the women of Rome would agree with you on that particular custom. Today he also becomes an official citizen. It is a very important day in a man's life. This evening they will all return for what is called the Feast of Liberation."

"That explains why everyone around here seems so preoccupied," Jeff observed.

"Yes. Augustus, the master of the house, and Dovenia have spared no expense in this banquet," Secunda explained. "Come to the kitchen with me. You can help me in the final preparations."

The kitchen looked a great deal like the kitchens they knew back home, with the exception being there were no modern conveniences. The large oven was heated by fire, and pots and pans hung from a great many cupboards. The ample counter space was covered with platters of beautifully prepared foods.

As they entered, Jeff took a closer look at one of the platters. "Hey, look, Gennie, they've got Jell-O, but it's clear!"

"Jell-O?" Secunda said. "I am not familiar with that, but those are jellyfish."

"What!" Gennie said, looking horrified at the glistening translucent blobs. "Jellyfish-like-from-the-beach jellyfish?"

"Oh, yes," Secunda said. "They are a great delicacy, and very expensive as well."

"Where we come from, they're considered gross!" Jeff said.

Secunda laughed. "Let me read to you what tonight's three courses will include. It is the finest menu I have ever seen. Every item is a rare treat acquired by Augustus at a great cost!" Secunda took a large sheet of papyrus from one of the countertops.

"First, we will be serving a number of appetizers—jellyfish and eggs, and sow's udders stuffed with salted sea urchins," Secunda began.

"Gross!" Gennie said.

"What are udders?" Jeff asked innocently.

"It's the part of the cow you pull to get milk!" Gennie blurted out, purposely trying to shock her younger brother,

"Only this is from a pig," Secunda corrected Gennie.

"That's twisted!" Jeff concluded.

"They're really quite delicious," Secunda said. "We'll also have boiled tree fungi with peppered fish sauce."

Gennie and Jeff made sour faces at each other. Secunda continued, "As well as patina of brains cooked with milk and eggs."

"Brains! Now I know you're joking," Jeff said.

"Would you care to try some?" she asked her two visitors. Secunda pointed to a platter sporting a dozen gray-brown glistening mounds.

"No!" the two said in unison.

"I think you'll find the main courses more traditional."

Gennie and Jeff looked suspicious.

"We have pork stuffed with pine kernels; deer roasted with onion sauce; boiled ostrich with Jericho dates; turtle dove boiled in its feathers," Secunda continued.

"Sick!" Gennie exclaimed.

"And roast parrot," Secunda finished.

"I'll bet that one tastes like crackers, Gennie," Jeff said with an impish look in his eye. "Get it, Gennie? 'Polly wants a cracker'."

"Very funny, Jeff," Gennie answered sarcastically.

"Would you like to hear what we'll have for dessert?" Secunda asked.

"I've heard enough," Genie replied.

"We don't have to eat that stuff tonight, do we?" Jeff asked.

"I am used to simpler fare as well," Secunda smiled. "You

may dine with me tonight in the kitchen. I have bread with honey and olives, if you prefer."

"Yes!" Jeff told her.

"Fine. Now we must return to work," Secunda commanded. "Jeff, we need more firewood from the pile outside, and, Gennie, you can help me with these two large platters."

CHAPTER 18

The Trap Is Sprung

It was early evening when Marcus's celebratory group returned. Altogether, nine people would attend the banquet—Augustus and Dovenia, Marcus and "charming" Androne, three of Marcus's friends, and Gracchus Tacitus, Augustus's employer, and his wife.

As the guests arrived, Gennie's task was to remove their sandals and wash their feet with a warm, wet, soapy washcloth. It was a demeaning task made even worse by the fact that several of Marcus's friends had not washed their feet for quite some time.

Augustus's employer, Gracchus, tottered in

with his wife. Although Gracchus was in his mid-70s, very old for the time, he had retained a youthful twinkle in his eyes and a spring in his step. Tonight, Augustus noticed that for the first time, Gracchus looked every bit his age. He seemed more tired than usual, and his face was a pale, ashen color.

All the dinner guests except Androne gathered in the atrium and casually talked among themselves. At last, Androne appeared. She had waited in her room until just the right moment so she could make a grand entrance. Even Gennie had to admit Androne's toga was by far the most beautiful. It caught and reflected the light like silk. Its intricate trim shimmered like gold. Androne's bright auburn hair had been carefully sculpted in a fashion to only reveal her tiny face.

But it was particularly disgusting to Gennie to watch as Androne giggled and coyly flitted about Sirocles, a handsome friend of Marcus.

The group leisurely strolled to the dining room in anticipation of the feast Secunda had prepared and for which Augustus had paid so dearly. They each took their places upon the opulent couches, and reclined on their left elbows, striking a pose they would keep for most of the night. Secunda wheeled in small carts of food, so the pampered diners rarely had to move.

Gennie patiently waited in the kitchen, talking to Jeff. After an hour or so, Secunda returned and told Gennie the guests had finished the appetizers and it was time for her to wash their hands.

"Begin with Gracchus's wife, then Dovenia, then Gracchus, next Marcus, then Androne, then Augustus, and finally Sirocles and the other friends of Marcus," Secunda explained. "The order is very important. As you approach them, they will offer you their hands for you to clean with the washcloth. It's really quite easy."

"Okay," Gennie said, and repeated Secunda's instructions in

perfect order.

"You are a quick learner," Secunda said. "I will be in the dining room standing by the door. If you should forget, just look to me and I will point out who to attend to next."

"Thanks," Gennie said, leaving the kitchen with several wet washcloths in hand.

Gennie began washing the guests' greasy hands.

Without napkins or utensils, they definitely needed the cleaning. Starting with Gracchus's wife, Gennie proceeded in the order Secunda had suggested. Gennie noticed that Androne had made sure to sit on the couch nearest to Sirocles. Although Sirocles preferred to talk to Marcus, Androne continually tried to enter their conversation.

Finally, while Gennie was cleaning Sirocles's hands, Gracchus's wife remarked, "Dovenia, I see you have a new household servant."

Androne interrupted, not allowing her mother to respond.

"No, this is a visitor from Gaul," Androne said with an air of superiority.

"A distant cousin," Augustus corrected.

"Yes, very distant," Androne said smugly. "And from what I can tell, never has there been a more backward place in all the world!"

Several of the guests laughed.

"But I must say," Augustus commented, "Gennie has a good head for business. That is rare these days."

"Gennie. Is that your name?" Sirocles asked quietly as Gennie finished washing his hands.

"Yes," Gennie answered.

"That is a pretty name," Sirocles said kindly. Gennie blushed, embarrassed by the young man's attention. Androne, however, was not amused. She was livid. Androne had been trying all evening to gain Sirocles's attention, and she was not about to be upstaged by this beggar from Gaul. Androne would fix Gennie. That is what Androne was very good at.

"Cousin dear," Androne said in her syrupy sweet voice, which immediately put Gennie on guard. "Please hand me that platter of ostrich. It is nearer to you than it is to me." Secunda looked nervously from across the room suspecting Androne was up to something.

Gennie set down her washcloths and lifted the heavy platter with bowls of boiled ostrich. She carefully held the large tray in front of Androne so she could take one of the bowls. But as she reached for a bowl, Androne suddenly pushed down hard on the front of the platter. The tray tilted towards Androne, and all the bowls of ostrich and sauce spilled onto the couch. Androne had been cunning enough to sit up just as the ostrich slid from the platter. Not a drop had soiled her new toga.

"You clumsy oaf," Androne shrieked. "Look what you've done! You did that on purpose!"

"But you tipped it," Gennie protested.

"Mother! She did this deliberately. She tried to cover me with food, and now she has absolutely ruined the couch!" Androne whined.

"That's not true!" Gennie objected. "You made me spill it!"

"Gennie!" Dovenia's voice cut above the others. "That is quite enough! Go into the kitchen for the remainder of the banquet! Secunda can wash our hands since you do not seem capable of even the most basic of tasks. When our guests leave, you will attend to their sandals at the door. I will discuss this with you later!"

As Gennie turned to leave the room, she could hear Androne's honey-sweet voice. "My couch is an absolute mess! Sirocles, do you mind if I share your couch?"

CHAPTER 19

Dovenia's Wrath

Gracchus walked slowly and unsteadily toward the door. He leaned heavily upon his wife for support. His face seemed to have grown even grayer and his manner even more frail over the course of the evening. Gennie carefully helped the old man with his sandals. Gracchus was the only guest who actually needed help, and Gennie was glad to give it.

"Dovenia, it was a wonderful banquet," Gracchus said weakly. "Perhaps the finest I've ever attended. A remarkable feast!"

"Thank you, Gracchus, that is most kind of you," Dovenia replied warmly. "If you enjoyed the evening then all our labors were well spent."

☙ Chapter Nineteen ☙

Gracchus turned his attention to Augustus. "You have a fine wife, Augustus. You are a lucky man. Tell me friend, when I see the luxuries of your household, I am amazed! You have prospered far beyond any of my other employees. How did you come by all this?"

"If one is shrewd and purchases wisely, much can be accomplished," Augustus said proudly.

"That gives me great comfort," Gracchus said. "I know I shall never have to worry about your well-being. You have done well indeed, Augustus!"

Augustus smiled at his wife. Gracchus placed a frail hand upon Augustus's shoulder. "Tomorrow I am having a special gathering of all my employees at the trading company. I have some news for everyone. I would have told you tonight, but Dovenia would never have forgiven me if I brought up business in the midst of Marcus's celebration." Gracchus coughed uncontrollably.

"Are you all right?" Dovenia asked.

"Yes, yes, just something I have picked up today," he said in a small voice. "I shall explain that tomorrow, as well. We will meet in our offices when the sundial shows 9 o'clock. Good night, Dovenia. Good night, Augustus."

Gracchus took one last look around the opulent entryway.

"Yes, you have done very well, Augustus. You should be proud of yourself."

"Thank you, Gracchus. Good night," Augustus said, and he slowly closed the door behind them.

"I have never seen Gracchus looking so poorly," Dovenia said sadly. "His advanced age is beginning to tell upon him."

Augustus chuckled to himself.

"What is it?" his wife asked.

"Don't you see?" Augustus said with a smile. "Tonight he comes to our household ill and stricken, and tomorrow there is to be a special meeting at the office."

"Perhaps I don't see," Dovenia said.

"His health has finally gotten the better of him. Tomorrow he will announce that he is stepping aside in the running of the company," Augustus said excitedly. "I am sure of it. And you know what that means?"

"It could mean a great many things," his wife answered carefully.

"He will retire and name his successor," Augustus said breathlessly. "Who better than to assume his role as head of the company than I?"

"But are there not others?" Dovenia questioned.

"None who have been in his employ for as long as I. None who have worked as hard as I. But more importantly, did you not hear Gracchus tonight?" Augustus said. "He was impressed with the riches of our household. Impressed by my shrewdness."

"I suppose so..." Dovenia said cautiously.

"The position is as good as mine!" Augustus exclaimed. "That will mean a raise in pay. And in time, if I am clever, I can acquire the trading company itself. Gracchus will soon lose interest in the enterprise."

Augustus laughed happily.

"If there had been any doubts in his mind, tonight washed them away! The lavish banquet, our beautiful furnishings, even our fine robes, all convinced him that I am the type of man who should be running his company!"

"He clearly was impressed by the house," Dovenia agreed. "And the banquet delicacies were a work of art! But I feel sorry for old Gracchus. He has been kind to us these many years."

"Yes, yes, of course. I feel sorry for him, too," Augustus said in an unconvincing tone. "But we cannot question the hands of the fates. Gennie, since you and Jeff inquired about wealth and attaining riches, I think it would be a good lesson for you to accompany me tomorrow to the trading company for Gracchus's announcement of my promotion. Tomorrow you will learn a great deal. Now I must tell Marcus and Androne this wonderful news!"

Augustus hurried back through the house to find his son and daughter.

Dovenia turned to Gennie, her expression hard and angry.

"Go to the kitchen and help Secunda clean up from the banquet. Young Gennie, while you are a guest in this house, I expect you to act as one. Your behavior toward Androne tonight was inexcusable! She is of a sensitive and delicate nature, and your actions tonight upset her. If you were not a relative, I would turn you out into the street. Tomorrow upon your return from the trading house, I have a special job for you."

Gennie stormed into the kitchen where Jeff had been helping Secunda most of the evening. Every available countertop was covered with dirty pots, pans, and dishes. Jeff was scraping what little food was left into a drainage hole in the floor.

"I'm so mad at her!" Gennie announced angrily.

"Who?" Jeff asked.

"Androne, that's who!" Gennie exploded. "She's such a phony suck-up!" Gennie's eyes were red and welling up with tears. Washing everyone's feet had been humiliating enough, but she had been berated by Dovenia in front of everyone and was going to be punished for something that was Androne's fault!

"This is a stupid family to have to stay with!" she said.

"We have to, Gennie," Jeff reminded her. "This is where Mortimer said we'd find the Second Pillar. We have to stay!"

"I know," Gennie said wiping her eyes. "She's just such a snot!"

"I know how you feel," Secunda kindly said, putting an arm around Gennie's shoulder to console her. "She's the most spoiled child I've ever met. I've seen her do this before. She's terrible to everyone, but she's absolutely evil around other girls, like a big spider."

"But if it makes you feel better, I'll tell you a secret," Secunda said quietly. Both Gennie and Jeff perked up. "The little empress is not nearly so perfect as she'd have us all think. Have you not wondered why she has her hair done in such a curious fashion, so that all but her face is hidden?"

"No," Jeff answered honestly.

"It looks stupid!" Gennie said, still angry.

"I'll tell you," Secunda said, leaning forward and speaking in a whisper. "It's her ears! They're the biggest I've ever seen on man or woman. The first time I accidentally saw them, I thought of Hannibal's elephants! And she was fuming mad that I had seen them! I'll tell you," she continued. "Augustus will have to provide a huge dowry once Androne's suitors see those wings of hers!"

Normally Gennie and Jeff didn't gossip a great deal, but Secunda's tale brought a wide smile to both their faces.

"Cheer up. Your parents will be here in a few days, will they not?" Secunda asked.

"Yes," Jeff answered tentatively.

"Well then, you won't have to put up with her much longer, will you?" Secunda said.

"No," Gennie conceded.

"Let's forget about this for tonight," Secunda urged. "I still need some help with all these dishes. Can I count on your help a while longer?"

"Yes," they answered together.

"Good!" Secunda handed each of them a wooden bucket and instructed them to go outside to the well to draw water for the dish washing. Outside, Gennie and Jeff discussed their progress in finding the Second Pillar.

"Jeff, I may have found the next secret," Gennie whispered.

"What is it?" Jeff eagerly asked.

"Augustus's boss came to dinner. He's really old and sick," Gennie explained. "Augustus thinks he's going to get a big promotion from the old man tomorrow. He said we could come along with him to the company where he works."

"So you think it's Augustus?"

"Either that or it might be the old man, Gracchus something," Gennie reasoned.

"Remember how Augustus said he'd built up the business? And it sounds like he has a lot of money!"

"Good work, Gennie!" Jeff said approvingly.

"Hurry up with that water!" Secunda's voice called out.

The two stopped their conversation and hurried back to the kitchen.

CHAPTER 20

Augustus's Promotion

The streets leading to the trading company were crowded with citizens. On several occasions, men stopped Augustus to make comments that confirmed his suspicions.

"Good morning, Augustus. I heard the news about Gracchus. I'm sorry. He is a good man," or "Give my regards to Gracchus," or "Sorry to hear about Gracchus."

The office of Gracchus's Trading House was in a small building near a tiny plaza. As Augustus, Gennie, and Jeff approached the door, they encountered Tirocles.

"Good morning, Tirocles!" Augustus said.

Confident of his upcoming promotion, Augustus was full of enthusiasm and energy.

"You seem in unusually good spirits this morning," Tirocles observed.

"This is a great day!" Augustus said. "You remember my cousin's children, Gennie and Jeff?"

"Yes, the ones who were so interested in money," Tirocles remembered. "How are you enjoying your trip from Gaul?"

"Great!" Jeff said.

"Okay," Gennie said, much less enthusiastically. Her mind was not on Augustus's promotion. Gennie wondered what *special job* Androne had arranged for them by manipulating Dovenia.

"I thought it would be instructional to bring them along to this meeting," Augustus told Tirocles.

"Really," Tirocles said with a puzzled look. "I would think they would be bored by all this talk of business."

"Well, I suspect this will be a memorable meeting," Augustus said knowingly. "Old Gracchus hinted to me that he will be announcing something important this morning."

"Yes, I have heard rumors, too," Tirocles said, opening the door so the three could enter before him. "I must confess, Augustus, you have more courage than I expected."

Augustus looked back toward Tirocles, confused by the strange comment. Perhaps poor Tirocles thought it took great bravery to run such a company. Well, that is why he shall always remain clerk, thought Augustus.

The dozen men crowded in the office's main room, with the exception of Augustus and Tirocles, chattered with one another, speculating on the reason for the special meeting. Augustus was too busy greeting everyone to listen to the others. Tirocles stood silently in the corner, watching Augustus.

Gracchus slowly entered the room, looking very old and tired. His walk had lost its characteristic spring. Every step seemed to be a strain. The gathering quieted as the old man shuffled to the center of the room.

"Thank you, all of you, for coming on such short notice," Gracchus said, looking about the room at the familiar faces. He stopped upon Gennie and Jeff.

"I see we have visitors with Augustus," he smiled. "Augustus, would it not be better for these two to play outside while we all discuss business?"

"I would like them to stay," Augustus told Gracchus.

"Very well," Gracchus said wearily. "I think some of you already know what I'm about to say. I have known most of you many years. Some longer than others." He looked at Augustus. "That is what makes this so hard for me. You have all been good, loyal employees. I suppose things always change and we must expect changes. That is why I must announce..."

"That I am promoting Augustus," Augustus said softly under his breath.

"...that I cannot pay you any longer. The trading company is in ruin!" Gracchus finished.

"What!" Augustus exploded. Gracchus's words struck him like a blow to the stomach.

"Are you in some sort of trouble Gracchus? Is there anything we can do?" Tirocles offered. Others made similar offers.

"What do you mean you cannot pay me?" Augustus shouted accusingly. "What have you done to the firm? What has happened?"

"Yesterday I received the word," Gracchus said sadly. "Our three ships, all of our ships, bound from Alexandria and loaded with grain were attacked and looted last week by Aegean pirates. The cargo was lost, the ships burned and sunk. I fear many crew lost their lives as well."

Gracchus's concern was genuine.

"But that was everything!" Augustus gasped, trying to contain himself. "We are wiped out! What are we to do?"

Augustus's heart was racing. It was hard for him to breathe.

"I am glad that at least you, Augustus, have prospered and this will be of little concern," Gracchus said.

"But, but..." Augustus stammered.

"I am terribly sorry. It was my doing. If our ships had slipped past the pirates, it would have been our richest year ever. But that obviously did not occur," Gracchus said. All those in the room were shocked by the terrible events, but Augustus was clearly the hardest hit.

"I shall be returning to the country," Gracchus began. "I must warn you, word of my ruin has spread quite quickly. Perhaps that will make it easier for you to find new employment.

"I am truly sorry," Gracchus said honestly.

Gracchus turned and, without so much as a final good-bye, left the office.

CHAPTER 21

The Passageway

When the three returned from Gracchus's office, Augustus was still in a state of shock. Augustus tried to mask his concern from the children, but to no avail. He barely spoke on the way home. He was deeply lost in thought and had a frightened look in his eyes. Upon entering the household, Augustus announced he had to speak with Dovenia at once.

"But I must attend to Gennie," Dovenia protested. "She needs to be punished for her unacceptable behavior last night."

"This is important!" Augustus shouted.

Androne had been eavesdropping from the atrium. "I will show her the drain, Mother," she said. "She knows it is by your bidding."

"Let Androne attend to that matter," Augustus said impatiently. "I need to talk with you now!"

"All right. Gennie, go with Androne. She will show you the job that must be done," Dovenia instructed. "And let me tell you, young lady, any more behavior like last night and it will not matter whose cousin you are. I will let you and your brother wander the streets of Rome!"

She walked off with Augustus hurrying her along.

"Well, dear cousin," Androne said in her sickly sweet voice. "Follow me."

She led Gennie and Jeff outside the house to a small opening between two walls. The narrow passageway gave off a foul odor.

"It stinks in there!" Jeff said. "What is it?"

"Gennie will be only too happy to tell you when she comes back out," Androne said, her voice dripping with honey. She handed Gennie a large wooden scrub brush.

"At the back of this passageway, there is a drain that has become blocked. All you need to do is crawl back there and unclog it," she said smugly.

Many, many years earlier, long before Augustus ever held title to the house, it had been two smaller houses. At some point, they had been joined to make one large house. But the narrow alleyway, four feet high and eighteen inches wide, between the two houses had never been joined. It still was used for the purpose it had served decades earlier—an open drainage system for all the toilets, kitchen waste, and used bath water of the house.

In this dark passageway all manner of waste, both human and inorganic, ran together, forming a putrid liquid sludge. The waste ran the full length of the house, then down a drain and into the city's crude sewage system. Every year or so, the drain clogged at the closed end of the passageway. Augustus hired the most desperate of laborers to crawl through the darkness, through the sewage runoff, and unclog the drain with their bare hands.

It was the most vile and hideous of tasks. Many of the laborers became ill within moments of entering the space. This was the task that Dovenia, spurred on by Androne, had selected as punishment for Gennie. For someone as fastidious as Gennie, this was a nightmare.

"I'm told it's not a pleasant job, but you finally have a task equal to your abilities," Androne said cruelly.

"Forget it!" Gennie said angrily, throwing the brush to the ground by Androne's feet. "This is all your fault! I didn't spill the food; you did! You can't order me around like some sort of slave!"

Androne's voice lost its sweetness and became hard. "If you refuse, I'll tell my Mother," she hissed. "She said she'd throw you out, and I'll see to it that she does! It's about time you learned how to talk to your superiors! You're nothing but a plain and stupid country girl, better suited for a servant's life! Don't clear the drain, I don't care. I'll be rid of you for good then. Either way, I'll enjoy it a great deal!"

Androne kicked the brush back towards Gennie. She turned and walked away, humming a cheerful tune.

"This isn't fair!" Gennie said. "She is such a jerk. Can't anybody else see what a phony she is?"

"We've only got one more day to go, Gennie," Jeff said, trying to sound encouraging. "That's all. Once we find out what the Second Pillar is, we'll never have to see her again!"

"I know," Gennie said, reluctantly picking up the brush. "It's just so unfair!"

Gennie got down on her hands and knees and started into the rancid alleyway. She stopped only six feet in. Jeff could see her feet.

She was still, until finally Jeff saw her beginning to back out.

She looked terrible. Her face was white and covered with tears. She was half crying, half-gagging. She was shaking with repulsion. "I can't do it," she cried. "I hate her! Look at me, I'm covered with this stuff."

Gennie's arms and legs were covered with foul slime.

"It's not fair," she said tearfully. "Mortimer never said we'd have to do something like this!"

Jeff looked at his sister a long while, then at the narrow alleyway, then back at Gennie.

"I'll do it," Jeff reluctantly volunteered.

"What?"

"I'll do it, Gennie. We have to, or we'll never find the Second Pillar, and then we'll be stuck here forever."

"I know. Will you really do it?" she said, wiping her eyes with the clean sleeve of her gown.

"It's my turn," Jeff said. "You had to wash everybody's feet last night."

"It really, really stinks in there," she advised her brother.

"I know." He wrapped the excess material from his robes around his nose and mouth as an impromptu gas mask.

"Give me the brush," he said with a muffled voice.

She handed it to him. Gennie was standing by, arms outstretched, repulsed by the foul sludge that covered her.

"You don't have to wait here," Jeff said generously. "You can go get cleaned up. I'm okay."

"Okay," she said quietly, and walked off as Jeff tentatively crouched down and entered the passageway.

Even with the cloth wrapped around his nose, the smell nearly gagged Jeff. His eyes watered and tears ran down his face from the pungent air. He could feel the lukewarm sludge all around his hands and feet as he crawled along the alleyway. And all the while, it became darker and darker.

Gennie came around the corner of the bath and nearly ran into Androne coming out. Androne had just finished her own bath. She was wrapped in a long towel, and held another wrapped around her hair.

"What are you doing here?" Androne asked, surprised to see Gennie so soon. "You were supposed to clean the drain!"

"I'm done with that," Gennie fibbed. "It only took me a minute. Don't tell me you thought that was a hard job?"

"You liar!" Androne sneered. "You couldn't have gone down in there already! Oh well, Mother will just make you do it later today."

"Well, if I didn't go down, you won't mind if I help you with your towels!" Gennie reached out as if to grab Androne, her hands and arms covered with foul-smelling sludge.

"Stay away from me, you pig! " Androne spat, and jumped out of Gennie's way. But as she jumped away, the towel atop her head fell to the ground. Androne's bright auburn hair was wet and slicked back, fully exposing her prominent ears. Gennie stopped in her tracks.

"Whoa!" Gennie said. "Those are huge!"

"Shut up, you filthy beggar!" Androne snapped. She hurriedly picked up the towel and covered her head in one rapid motion.

"You'll be sorry about this!" Androne threatened, as she ran from the room.

CHAPTER 22

The Money Lenders

While Jeff was crawling forward in the putrid little alleyway, he made a useful discovery. The walls, made of the worst possible construction, were so thin that Jeff could hear any conversation taking place within the house. As he passed under one room after another, faint voices grew louder and then faded as he passed. Not only could he hear talking, but every room contained a crack or crevice with which to spy inside.

"This is awesome!" he said quietly to himself. "It's like being backstage at a play. I can spy on everybody in the house!"

But the knowledge came at a high price. His arms and legs had become covered in foul, lukewarm slime.

One particular set of voices caught Jeff's attention—Augustus and Dovenia. It was clear they were arguing, and Jeff heard one of them mention *money*. He crawled along the passageway until he found a small crack that gave him a view into Augustus's office, the room in which he and Gennie had asked Augustus about money only yesterday. Jeff could see everything inside, including Augustus and Dovenia.

"But how could the old fool lose everything?" Dovenia shouted.

"I don't know," Augustus said wearily. "He built the company by taking chances. Luck has finally turned against us."

"Luck! Luck has nothing to do with it!" Dovenia angrily said. "And what of us? You have borrowed and borrowed and borrowed, always telling me not to worry, not to concern myself with matters of business, that you would handle everything. And now where has this gotten us?"

There was a faint knock at the door.

"Come in," Augustus said.

Secunda abruptly opened the door. Jeff could see she looked troubled.

"I'm sorry, Master Augustus. I tried to make them wait but..." Before Secunda could finish, two men pushed past her into the room. One man was small and thin, with nervous rodent-like eyes that darted about the room. The other was tall and muscular. Jeff took him to be a soldier or fighter. He had a patch over one useless eye and a large red scar, which angled down across the entire length of his face. The small one spoke.

"Well, well, well, Augustus. Lucius and I are very pleased to find you at home. Are we not Lucius?"

The large man merely grunted his approval.

"Who are these men?" Dovenia asked her husband.

"This is Romulens," Augustus said, referring to the small man. "I don't know the other."

"His name is Lucius," Romulens said. "He is a business associate of mine. You may have heard of him. He was a gladiator for many years until I bought him. In the arena, he was known as The Butcher."

"What business do you have with my husband in my house?" Dovenia asked defensively.

"Ah, this must be the lovely Dovenia," Romulens hissed. "Augustus has spoken much of you. I must compliment you on the many beautiful furnishings within these walls."

"Thank you, but Augustus and I are discussing something of importance. Perhaps you could return in an hour or so?" Dovenia asked firmly, but politely.

"You mean come back to *my* house," Romulens sneered.

"Your house?" Dovenia looked fearful for the first time. "What does he mean by that, Augustus?"

"I am sorry my dear. Romulens is a money lender," Augustus answered.

Dovenia looked frightened now, fully realizing their desperate situation.

"Please let me speak with them in private, Dovenia," Augustus said. "We will speak more of this later."

"All right," Dovenia said, "I will honor your request. We will speak after these two have gone."

She and Secunda left the room and closed the door behind them.

"You disappoint me, Augustus," Romulens said. "After all the many years that we have conducted business together, you now refer

to me as merely a lender of coin? Have we not broken bread together? Have I not been your best of friends when you sought ever
more money for your luxurious lifestyle? Why just a week ago I was
a man of 'great character' when I loaned you the denarii for your
son's liberation feast. And now I am but a money lender?"

"What is it you want, Romulens?" Augustus asked coolly.

"I think you know what I want. Word has spread throughout
the city that Gracchus's business has failed. This concerns me,"
Romulens said, his eyes narrowing. "How am I to be repaid now
that you have no position?"

"You will be repaid. I just need a little time," Augustus pleaded.

"You are a fool, Augustus!" Romulens said angrily. "And now
you have made a fool out of me, as well. Your loss was the loss of *my*
money!"

All the while, Lucius picked up things from Augustus's desk,
clumsily examining them and replacing them.

"Let me teach him a lesson, Master Romulens. I would like to
show him something of the arena," the brute said with a twisted
smile.

Augustus was visibly shaken at the thought of Romulens turning this thug against him.

"You see, Augustus," Romulens said in a false whisper, "I would
personally like to grant you more time, but Lucius here is in charge
of my customers who are late with their payments. And he is most
insistent."

Lucius grinned again at the thought of doing great physical harm
to Augustus.

"But I only need a little more time, Romulens," Augustus begged.
"You will get more denarii returned if you are patient. I'm sure I
can raise the money for you."

"Why should I wait? The note you signed said I could call your debt whenever it suited me. And it suits me now," Romulens said with a smile. "Besides, your reputation is well-known among all the money lenders. No one will loan you more money."

"But I can get work and repay you from my wages!" Augustus said.

Romulens laughed cruelly. "And who would hire a man such as yourself? You have become a pompous ass. Perhaps you can start over as a clerk, but a clerk's wages will never repay what you now owe me."

"But I just need a little more time," Augustus pleaded.

"Tomorrow morning we shall begin to seize what possessions of yours might be sold," Romulens said, matter-of-factly. "Your chariot and your furniture will do for a start."

"And what then?" Augustus asked fearfully.

"You know Senatorial Law as well as I, Augustus, for debtors who cannot pay," Romulens said. "You knew the penalties when you signed my note."

"No! Not servitude!" Augustus protested. "Think of my family. Please, I beg of you."

"You should have thought of that when you spent my money so freely and foolishly, Augustus. I have already made the arrangements. Tomorrow evening you will have yet another special gathering in your home, although this one will not prove so enjoyable!" Romulens threatened. "And if you should think of running away, Lucius will be standing guard outside in the street. Let us go, Lucius."

As the two left, Lucius passed close by Augustus and quietly said, with a strange grin, "I hope you do try and run!"

After they left, Augustus collapsed into a chair from exhaustion and fear, aghast at the fate he had brought upon his family and household.

Below, Jeff had seen and heard enough. He began to crawl back through the filthy waste to the drain, anxious to leave this stench rapidly and tell his sister all that he had overheard.

Once outside the house, Lucius commented, "That went well, Master Romulens."

"Compared to what, Lucius? Will he try to flee for his life? No, he is too cowardly and bound to his family. Can he repay me? No, he is a fool when it comes to money. And whose loss is it, Lucius? Now it is both of ours, Augustus's and mine. He drank and ate at my expense and now he will ply his skills on a slave ship. I doubt he will fetch a price equal to all that I have lent him. We both lose, Lucius, he and I," Romulens lectured his associate. "But mark my words, Lucius, his banquet was his greatest folly. The man who borrows for what he passes the next day is the greatest fool of all!"

After dinner, Gennie and Jeff talked quietly in their room about what they'd observed that day. Gennie told Jeff about her unpleasant encounter with Androne.

"Jeff," she whispered in a conspiratorial tone. "You should see her ears! Secunda was right! They're huge! I mean she could be in the circus with them!"

They both laughed. It was the first time since they'd started their quest for the Three Pillars that they'd had a really good laugh.

Jeff explained the conversation he overheard from the passageway. It had taken most of the afternoon to wash off the stench. He told Gennie what Augustus and Dovenia had talked about, about the money lenders, and how Augustus was in trouble. Jeff didn't fully understand what was going to happen next.

"It sounded like Augustus is going to wind up being a slave or something," Jeff said. "But I didn't really get it."

"Tomorrow we can ask Secunda," Gennie suggested. "She'll know."

"One thing for sure," Jeff added. "Borrowing isn't the Second Pillar! Augustus isn't going to wind up with anything. He's broke!"

"I know," Gennie agreed. "Tomorrow's our last day, too. I'm starting to worry again. I mean there's nobody else around besides the family."

"Mr. Mortimer said we'd find the Second Pillar *within the house*," Jeff said. "I guess we just have to wait."

"I guess so," Gennie concluded.

They hopped into their respective beds across the room from one another. Jeff blew out the oil lamp and the room filled with darkness. Several minutes passed in silence.

"Jeff, are you awake?" Gennie whispered.

"Yeah," he answered quietly.

"Thanks for going in there for me today," she said.

"It's okay," he answered.

"Good night, Jeff," Gennie said and rolled over.

"Good night," Jeff said, pulling the covers around himself.

Heartfelt gratitude from an older sister was rare. Jeff grinned to himself in the darkness as he nodded off to sleep.

CHAPTER 23

Indentured Servitude

Gennie and Jeff were abruptly awakened at dawn when two burly workers entered their room.

"Get out of bed!" one of them commanded. "We need to move all this out this morning!"

"We can come back for the beds later. For now, let's move everything else into the carts," the second man said, as if Gennie and Jeff weren't even in the room. The two children quickly put cloaks on over the togas they'd slept in and headed toward the kitchen in search of Secunda.

"What's going on?" Jeff asked Secunda. "No one will tell us what's happening."

"I've heard Dovenia crying," Gennie added. "And Augustus told us we would have to leave tonight."

"I hope your parents arrive soon from Gaul," Secunda said gravely. "The streets of Rome are not a friendly place for two such as yourselves."

"But what's going on?" Gennie insisted.

"Master Augustus has borrowed great sums of money," Secunda said. "Now he cannot repay it. According to Roman law, he and Marcus will be sold tonight into indentured servitude."

"What's that?" Jeff asked.

"Be thankful you do not have such laws in Gaul," Secunda said. "This evening, Augustus and Marcus will be sold, like cattle, to the highest bidder. They then must work as servants for whoever buys them until the purchase price is repaid."

"Why is Marcus included?" Gennie asked. "Wasn't it Augustus who borrowed the money?"

"Marcus is now sixteen," Secunda explained. "In the eyes of the law, he is a man, and must share responsibility for any debts of the household. It is sad for Marcus. Had his birthday been but a few days later, he would have escaped this fate."

"But it's not like they're going to prison or something," Jeff said. "How bad can it be?"

"Few in servitude ever regain freedom," Secunda said sadly. "Not only must you repay what was paid for you, but you must also repay all food and lodging while you are kept. Depending upon how much is paid for Augustus and Marcus, they will probably be servants for fifteen to twenty years!"

"That's terrible!" Gennie said.

"Marcus was sort of a jerk," Jeff observed. "But a whole lifetime of that, it's like being a slave!"

"True, it is just like being a slave."

"What will happen to Androne and her mom?" Jeff asked.

"They'll have to seek the charity of relatives and friends," Secunda said. "Otherwise, they'll be thrown into the streets to fend for themselves."

Secunda paused a moment and quickly glanced about the kitchen to make sure no one else was present. She lowered her voice.

"But that's not the worst of it," she said. "What the family fears most is the *Dark One!*"

"The Dark One?" Gennie repeated.

"Augustus's fall from power is not unique. Many in Rome have fallen because debt is so tempting, like a siren luring sailors on to the rocks. But lately, these servant auctions have been attended by a sinister man whose identity is unknown," Secunda continued in a hushed voice. "They say he wears a black robe with his hood drawn down to hide his features."

"So what?" Jeff said defiantly.

"In the last few months, at many of these auctions," Secunda explained, "this Dark One has appeared. There are rumors that he buys slaves for the salt mines. Another says his victims become galley slaves. And there are even more hideous rumors that I will not tell you. It is even whispered among the superstitious that he is death himself, buying souls for the underworld. But whatever he is, the servants he acquires are never seen or heard from again. His purchase is the same as a death sentence!"

Gennie and Jeff were silenced by Secunda's grim tale.

"But can't someone just bid more than him?" Jeff finally asked. "Is he so rich that no one can outbid him?"

"That is the tragedy in all this," Secunda answered. "This Dark One is feared by everyone! Because he is rumored to be so many terrible things, men are afraid to bid against him. Can you blame them?"

"I guess not," said Gennie.

"Indentured servitude is terrible, particularly for young Marcus. He is not to blame for his father's folly," Secunda said thoughtfully. "This evening when the auction begins, all present will be praying to the gods that this Dark One does not appear!"

Dovenia called for Secunda from another part of the house.

"I must return to my work," Secunda said, scurrying out of the kitchen. "Please tell no one what we have said."

"We won't," Jeff said. "We won't."

CHAPTER 24

The Dark One

As darkness descended upon ancient Rome, the little atrium in Augustus's house was crowded in anticipation of the impending auction. Nearly fifty people pushed their way into the center of the house. In truth, only six or seven of those people were seriously interested in bidding for Augustus or Marcus. While a few of those were curious neighbors, the vast majority were business and trades people who Augustus had slighted with his arrogance over the last three years. They were here to gloat at his misfortune.

Gennie and Jeff squeezed in and out of the crowd. So far so good! There was no sign of anyone dressed in a black, hooded robe. Romulens had hired soldiers to stand guard at the doorway to ensure an orderly evening without any outbursts. Near the soldiers stood Lucius, the ex-gladiator who now worked with Romulens.

A few minutes after the auction's scheduled start, Romulens walked to the front of the atrium. He stood on a small platform in the front of the courtyard, built to ensure all could easily see him as he conducted the auction.

"Good evening, my friends," Romulens said, surveying the crowded room with a smile. Normally Romulens did not enjoy these auctions. It meant one of his borrowers could not repay his debts. Usually the auction price fell far short of the amount he was due. But tonight might be different.

A large crowd was an excellent sign and usually made for spirited bidding. In the right atmosphere, these two men might fetch 50,000 or 60,000 denarii. Romulens might finish the evening with a handsome profit. That was a most pleasant thought.

"My name is Romulens. I am the auctioneer tonight," he said, as the crowd quieted down to listen. "I must say that these two men, known to many of you, are two of the finest I have had the unhappy task of turning over to servitude."

A rotund man close to Gennie and Jeff leaned over and whispered to his friend, "The windbag! He'd sell his own mother for two denarii. Why doesn't he just get on with it? I'm anxious to see how much the two fetch."

"You all know Augustus Diacus," Romulens continued. "A fine business man down on his luck. A shrewd merchant and calculator of numbers. He alone is worth perhaps 50,000 denarii."

"Not to me!" a woman shouted back, and the nervous crowd laughed.

"Ah, but there is yet another prize. Augustus's son, Marcus

Diocus. He has just turned sixteen. Stand up, Marcus!" he shouted.

Marcus and Augustus were seated off to the side of the atrium. Marcus stood slowly.

"Perhaps he doesn't look it, but he is strong as an ox, and will provide years and years of faithful service," Romulens said.

"It will be the first hard work the lazy boy has ever done," someone shouted.

"Together, these two are worth at least 100,000 denarii!" Romulens testified. Many smiled at the inflated value. Romulens hoped to inflate their worth as much as possible to inflate the bidding, and, in turn, inflate his purse.

The crowd blocked Jeff and Gennie's view.

"Have you seen anything yet?" Jeff asked.

"You mean our guy in black? No, I can see a little bit of the doorway from here," she said, straining her neck. "No one like that has come in yet."

"The bidding will start at 5,000 denarii," Romulens instructed the crowd. "Who will bid 5,000?"

Several hands shot into the air.

"I have 5,000," Romulens said, pointing to a thin wine merchant. "Do I hear 6,000?"

"Six thousand!" the proprietor of a gambling house called out.

"I have 6,000," Romulens said, pointing to the new bidder. "Do I hear 7,000?"

"Seven thousand," the wine merchant called out.

A weathered sea captain called out, "8,000!"

"Nine thousand!" the wine merchant shouted.

"Ten thousand!" the captain countered.

"I have 10,000 denarii," Romulens announced. "Please, you insult me and these two men. They are both in the prime of their lives. A pair such as this should be worth a small fortune."

"Eleven thousand!" the wine merchant yelled, waving his hand.

"I have 11,000 on the side," Romulens said, pointing to the merchant. "Do I hear 12?"

"Twelve thousand!" the gambling house owner called out.

"I hear 12,000," Romulens called out. "Come now, people, these two men..." Romulens stopped mid-sentence, frozen like stone. He gaped wide-eyed toward the rear of the atrium.

"What is wrong?" several voices questioned. "Why has he stopped?"

Gradually all eyes turned to the rear of the room. Standing near the doorway was a figure wearing a black cloak, with a large hood pulled low to hide his face.

"Twelve thousand and one denarii," the dark figure said loudly. No one in the atrium stirred. The auction was all but forgotten. Augustus's wife, bravely watching the grim proceedings from the doorway of her bedroom, broke down into tears upon seeing the dark figure and hearing him bid for her husband and son.

"Whoa," Jeff said. "That guy gives me the creeps!"

"No wonder everyone is afraid of him!" Gennie said.

"Curse the gods," Romulens muttered under his breath. He wiped sweat, which had suddenly appeared, off his brow. Here was the accursed Dark One he had heard about. Romulens had been told of other money lenders who had lost great sums of money because of this figure. People were so terrified of this man, that once his presence became known, all bidding stopped. A cruel twist of fate, thought Romulens.

"I bid 12,001 denarii!" the figure called out to Romulens. "Did you not hear me?"

Romulens was startled back to attention. The hooded figure

had only raised the last bid by a single denarius. Perhaps he could outsmart this mysterious stranger.

"I heard the bid at the rear of the room," Romulens said. "I'm sorry to say we are bidding in increments of 1,000 denarii. I cannot accept your bid!"

Everyone in the crowd was still turned around, eyes glued to the dark figure. He stepped closer to the crowd.

"I hear no objections from these others! Does anyone here object to my bidding in this manner?" the Dark One challenged in a deep voice. No one uttered a sound. All turned to Romulens to see how he would react.

Romulens wiped more sweat from his face. He wondered why it had suddenly become so hot.

"Well, of course, if there are no objections, I'm sure we can make an exception in this case," Romulens stammered. "All right, the bidding now stands at 12,001 denarii. Who shall make it 13,000?"

But all remained silent.

"How about 12,500? Come now, people. This is a great bargain! These two men are worth 30,000 denarii!" Romulens pleaded, but the room was quiet.

The thin wine merchant started to raise his hand to bid, but his wife seized hold of him in restraint.

"Are you mad?" she said to him in a loud whisper.

"But that's a wonderful bargain for those two," he told her.

"It is no bargain if you're in your grave!" she said. "Do you not see who stands at the rear of the room? It is the specter of death himself. What sort of fool am I married to?"

The wine merchant obediently lowered his hand.

"Surely someone wants these two fine servants. They will provide years and years of service!" Romulens begged the people. "Certainly they are worth a much higher bid!"

"It would appear I have the high bid," the dark figure said from the rear of the gathering.

The bidding stood at 12,001 denarii, a fraction of what Augustus and Marcus had borrowed from Romulens. It was no use, thought Romulens. No one dares bid against the Dark One.

"Very well," Romulens conceded. "Twelve thousand and one once, 12,001 twice, sold, for 12,001 denarii!"

Augustus turned to Marcus, whose eyes were filled with fear. "Forgive me, my son. I never meant to bring this upon you."

"I know," Marcus replied in a frightened voice.

There was no enthusiastic applause that typically followed a spirited bidding war. There was only the hurried shuffling of feet as the onlookers left as quickly as possible. As they filed out the atrium doorway, they stole quick glances at the darkly clad figure. The man stood motionless until everyone had departed.

Once all the people had left, the hooded figure slowly walked to Romulens. "Here is your money," the Dark One said. He counted out the 12,001 denarii in gold. Romulens angrily took the money and put it into his leather pouch.

"Your bargain has come at my expense, stranger," he said to the hooded figure.

"You have your money, now go," the figure ordered Romulens. "You have no more business here!"

Romulens paled at the threat.

"I was just leaving. The man and the boy are seated over there," he said, pointing across the atrium.

"I will collect my property shortly," the Dark One said.

He stepped uncommonly close to Romulens, their faces within

inches of one another. In an ominous voice, no louder than a whisper, the figure said, "Leave!"

As Romulens was departing with Lucius, he called back over his shoulder to Augustus, "You have cheated me, Augustus, but you cannot cheat death!"

Romulens laughed and was gone.

Augustus and Marcus sat on the far side of the atrium, dreading their hopeless future. The Dark One walked past Gennie and Jeff without so much as a word to the two of them. Augustus looked up toward the hidden face of the stranger.

"What is our fate?" Augustus asked. "The salt mines. Or pulling the oar of a pirate ship until we die?"

Augustus stood and looked upon his new owner. "Do not toy with us! What is our fate to be?"

A calm voice from behind the hood said, "I am granting you your freedom. You are free men!"

"What?" Augustus gasped.

Marcus sprang to his feet. "Do you speak the truth?"

The Dark One slowly pulled back his hood and let the long robe fall to the floor.

"It cannot be!" Augustus exclaimed.

"How can it be possible?" Marcus stammered.

"You! You are the Dark One?" Augustus gasped.

Standing before them was Tirocles, Augustus's loyal clerk.

CHAPTER 25

The Wisdom of Saving

Tirocles smiled. "No, but it proved useful to assume this role."

Augustus's gratitude had finally humbled him. He quietly asked, "Why, Tirocles? Why would you help me like this?"

"I have owed you a debt of gratitude ever since you suggested Gracchus hire me, eighteen years ago. That meant a great deal to me. I had promised myself I would help you if you ever needed it. Tonight you did," Tirocles said, looking Augustus in the eyes.

"You will have my lifelong gratitude, old friend. I'm afraid I have mistreated you these last three years," Augustus said.

Tirocles made no objection to Augusutus's confession. His silence confirmed that he had suffered from Augustus's conceit and arrogance.

"You and Marcus have your freedom," Tirocles said tiredly. "My debt to you is repaid."

"But where did you obtain 12,000 denarii?" Augustus asked. "Even I have never had so much money at one time!"

"From the first day I worked in the trading house for Gracchus," Tirocles began, "and every day thereafter, I set aside one-quarter of my pay. Before I considered the purchase of fine clothing, before I considered the purchase of delicious wine and foods, before I even considered the home that would shelter my family, I saved a portion of my pay. Before all else, I paid myself. Year after year after year that grew to a tremendous amount."

"And you, the *lowly clerk,*" Augustus said, shaking his head. "You have proven yourself far wiser than I, Tirocles. Now I have nothing."

"You have your freedom," Tirocles observed "Be thankful for that."

"Yes, and with that, a chance to start anew," Augustus said. "I must tell Dovenia and Androne. They will be as overjoyed as I at your generosity. Come, Marcus!"

Augustus ran off to find his wife and daughter, with Marcus following closely behind him.

Gennie and Jeff approached Tirocles. At last! Here was the Second Pillar—*saving!*

"Gennie and Jeff," Tirocles kindly addressed the two. "Several days ago you asked Augustus for his secret for attaining wealth. Do you remember?"

"Yes," Jeff said.

Chapter Twenty-Five

"Why didn't you tell us?" Gennie wondered.

"Would you have believed a humble clerk's opinion, compared to what you could see with your own eyes—the luxuries of this household?" he asked them.

"Probably not," Jeff admitted.

"The time was not right," Tirocles said. "Now it is. When I was a young boy, I had a curious dream. It was so vivid and true to life, that for many days I thought it had actually occurred. In my dream, a strange old man with a curious staff spoke to me."

"Mortimer!" Jeff and Gennie both said under their breath.

"The old man said that the difference between a life of happiness and a life of misery was one denarius," Tirocles said.

"One denarius, just one?" Jeff asked.

"Only one denarius," Tirocles confirmed. "He said if you spend one denarius *less* than you earn, you will have happiness. But if you spend one denarius *more* than you earn, it will lead to misery. And as you unfortunately saw, Augustus spent many, many, many more denarii than he earned."

"Why didn't Augustus save his money?" Gennie asked.

"To save, one must have the fortitude to delay some pleasures today for tomorrow. That is very hard for many people. It was very hard for Augustus," Tirocles observed. "To save, one must be willing to live *beneath* his means. Augustus lived *above* his means."

"But," Jeff began to speak then stopped.

"What is it?" Tirocles asked. "You may speak your mind."

"That was so much money!" Jeff observed. "I don't see how Augustus will ever be able to pay you back!"

"I don't expect he ever will," Tirocles admitted, surprising both Gennie and Jeff. "I could not desert an old friend, no matter how he has behaved of late. He has not gotten off so easy. He has his freedom, yes, but he is now bankrupt. He will not have such an easy time of it. He will suffer for many years for being so short-sighted."

"But now all your money is gone, too!" Gennie said.

"That is kind of you to be concerned," Tirocles smiled. "I have saved for many years. I have a great deal more. This was but a small portion of my wealth."

CHAPTER 26

Gennie's Fond Farewell

Jeff was the first to wake up in the middle of the night. He looked around the darkened room. Gennie was still sleeping. All was quiet throughout the house. Jeff gently shook Gennie by the shoulder.

"Gennie, Gennie, wake up! It's time to go," he said quietly.

"What, is it time already?" she said in a groggy voice.

"Yes, come on. Let's get out of here!" Jeff said.

"Oh my gosh! I nearly forgot!" Gennie said, leaping out of bed. "I'll be right back!" She rushed from the room.

"Gennie, we don't have any time!" Jeff called after her, but there was no response.

Jeff put on his sandals and walked into the atrium.

"Gennie!" he called in a loud whisper, but still she didn't answer.

Jeff looked down, shocked to see the silver fluorescent mist beginning to swirl about his feet! He was starting his return to the Chamber of Pillars, and Gennie was nowhere to be seen!

"Gennie!" he called loudly, no longer worried about waking anyone. Still no answer. The mist, spinning faster now, was up to his knees.

"Gennie!" he shouted as loud as he could. "You're going to be left behind!"

The gradually rising mist, whirling even faster, was now up to his waist.

He was about to step out of the mist to find Gennie when she appeared out of the darkness across the atrium.

"Coming!" she shouted. She bounded across the room to Jeff's side just as the mist rose to his shoulders.

"You almost blew it!" he scolded her. "What's so important? Did you want to get stuck here forever? Don't you want to get home?"

"Yes," Gennie said, her face beaming with a broad smile.

"So what's the big deal?" Jeff asked, irritated by Gennie's casual attitude about nearly being left behind.

As the fluorescent mist encircled them, Gennie held up a pair of kitchen shears in one hand, and a great deal of bright auburn hair in the other.

When the stars and mist subsided, Gennie and Jeff stood again in the cavernous hall, which contained the colossal Three Pillars of

Wealth. A smiling Mr. Mortimer greeted them.

"Back already?" he asked, pretending to be surprised.

"We were gone three days!" Jeff said.

"And it seemed like forever!" Gennie exclaimed.

"Ah, yes, of course, but remember, to those not traveling with you, it is as if you have not been gone at all," Mortimer reminded them. "Once more you have done well, my young students. Tell me of the Second Pillar."

"It's saving!" Gennie blurted out.

"Very true. Behold, the second great column reveals itself to you!" he said, pointing to one of the massive structures with his staff. At the base of the great pillar, letters slowly appeared in the stone: S-A-V-I-N-G. Gennie and Jeff touched the lettering, which looked as if it had been there all the time.

"And young Gennie," Mortimer smiled, "it would appear you have taken on the profession of a barber!"

Jeff and Gennie looked at each other and laughed.

"That was excellent, Gennie," Jeff congratulated his sister.

"The lesson you gave to Androne was well-deserved," the ancient man said. "But what of the lesson you two learned?"

"It was kind of confusing," Gennie said. "Augustus had such a strong desire to become rich, and he worked hard, so we thought he would lead us to the Second Pillar."

"But Tirocles the clerk was the smart one who saved his money," Jeff observed. "He just never talked about it like Augustus."

"Well observed," Mortimer told them. "Remember in your travels, the desire or the fire within to attain wealth is not always a loud and brilliant flame. It can be a silent, glowing ember. The desire is just as strong, but kept beneath the surface. Tirocles was wise. From every payment he received, he set aside a portion for himself. In this way, he accumulated a great deal of money."

"Unlike Augustus, who spent everything he had," Gennie said.

"He was spending *more* than he had, Gennie. Remember he was borrowing a ton of money," Jeff added.

"Yes, that was unfortunate," Mortimer said sadly. "Although Augustus had the desire for wealth, he lacked the foresight to hold onto it. Saving requires the discipline to delay gratification, to postpone the pleasures money could provide today, for the opportunities it can bring tomorrow. It is this, the Second Pillar of Wealth, which although best known among men…"

"And women," Gennie added.

"Yes," Mortimer smiled. "It is the best known among men *and* women, but it is the hardest to follow."

THE THIRD PILLAR

CHAPTER 27

The Shire of Worstecher

"Mr. Mortimer," Jeff said. "What if want to go home now?"

Gennie nodded in agreement.

"Go home?" Mr. Mortimer asked.

"Well, what more is there?" Jeff asked. "We know about having the *desire* to be wealthy, and how you have to *save*. Isn't that enough?"

Mr. Mortimer looked crestfallen.

"As I told you in the beginning, between each pillar you could return home at any time. And that is still true," the ancient man said. "Yet there is one pillar left, and there is much to be learned from it. It completes the circle. To come so far, and now fall short of the summit, would be unfortunate."

"No offense," Gennie said. "But it seems like we could become rich with just the first two pillars."

"Partially," Mr. Mortimer said thoughtfully. "But tell me, both of you, has this quest been only for yourselves? Have you traveled so far, risked so much, and overcome so many obstacles, simply for your own sake alone?"

Gennie and Jeff were silent.

"Or was it to help your parents?" Mr. Mortimer asked. "To find a way to eliminate the troubles that plague your household?"

"Yes," Gennie and Jeff both answered.

"The Third Pillar is that which pertains most to them," Mr. Mortimer said excitedly. "If you can successfully unravel this last and final secret, you will indeed be able to help your mother and father. But, as always, the choice is up to you. What do you say?"

Gennie and Jeff looked at one another.

"It *is* the last one," Gennie said to Jeff.

"And it *is* for Mom and Dad," Jeff reminded Gennie.

"Okay," Gennie said for both of them.

"Very well," Mortimer said. "You shall visit the shire of Worstecher. Seek out Waldor of Kelter. It is he, and the events of the next three days, that will help you discover the Third Pillar. Good luck!"

The flash of starlight swirled about the two and, for a third time, they sped off through time and space where the final puzzle awaited them.

Jeff and Gennie found themselves upon a dirt road. On one side of the road were thickly forested foothills, and on the other side was a broad valley of cottages and small farms. It was dusk. The sun was just setting behind a hillside. Both were struck at how everything was so green—the hills, the farmlands, everything.

They looked at each other's clothes. They both wore large loose-fitting shirts, cut from coarse brown burlap. They wore shorts of similar material. Their legs were covered with dark green tights that were a patchwork of holes and rips. They were dirty and splattered with mud from head to toe.

"Why does Mr. Mortimer always send us back with such terrible clothes?" Gennie wondered. Jeff paid little attention to his sister's complaints.

"Let's go to that house and ask if they know where we can find this Waldor guy," Jeff said, pointing to the closest cottage.

A tall fence of stone and splintered wood rails surrounded the cottage. Gennie began to walk around the fence, having spotted a gate. Jeff decided it would be much quicker to simply climb over the fence. Although only five feet tall, the fence was precarious and contained many sharp wooden spikes to discourage trespassers. Jeff easily scrambled to the top.

"Hey, Gennie!" he called. "It would be faster if you…"

At that instant, a portion of the ancient fence, unable to support Jeff's weight, gave way and collapsed. As Jeff fell to the ground, a sharp wooden spike lanced his right shin. He hit the ground gripping his right leg in pain.

"Oww! Gennie get help! I really hurt myself!" he called to his sister. His leg was now bleeding through his tight grasp.

Gennie raced to the closest cottage and banged upon the door. A middle-aged woman answered, "May I help you?"

"My brother fell off your fence and is hurt! Can you come help? Please," Gennie pleaded breathlessly.

"Of course, of course. Waldor," the woman said over her

shoulder. "Someone's been hurt."

The woman rushed out the door, followed by a bearded man. As they ran to Jeff's aid, Gennie realized that the woman had called the man "Waldor." This was the man Mr. Mortimer had told them to find. It was from this man they hoped to secure the secret of the Third Pillar. The woman bent down to look at Jeff's wound.

"I can't see anything in this light," she said to the man. "Carry him in so we may examine his injury in the light."

Waldor bent down, lifted Jeff easily, and carried him back into the house. He set him down upon a short, wooden table. The woman ripped away his dirty tights and carefully examined the wound. Waldor held a candle close to Jeff's leg. Gennie saw there were no electric lights in the cottage. Everything was lit with candles.

"This is not so bad," the woman said, greatly relieved. "The spike did not go far into his leg. He's very lucky! It looks much worse than it actually is."

"He bleeds a great deal for a small lad," Waldor commented.

The woman wiped the blood from the wound with a cloth. Jeff winced in pain. She wrapped Jeff's calf and shin tightly with a cloth bandage.

"There. You'll be as good as new in a week or two," she said.

"You'll have a nice scar upon your shin, but that will be your mark of courage," Waldor said to Jeff.

"Thank you," Jeff said weakly. He sat up slowly and carefully got down from the table. He tried to walk, but limped painfully when he put his full weight on the leg.

"We should take you two home," the woman remarked. "Where do you live? I don't recall seeing you in our village before."

"We're not from around here," Gennie told her. "We're from pretty far away."

"And what of your parents?" the woman asked. "Where might they be?"

"They're not here, either," Gennie said. Both Gennie and Jeff were saddened at the thought of their parents, so far away.

"Hmm," the man thought aloud. The man and woman exchanged puzzled looks. Finally, the woman spoke. "Well, then you shall stay with us tonight."

"But the contest…" Waldor started to interrupt, but the woman cut him off.

"You can't travel about in the dark, and your brother here with his bad leg. It's settled! You shall rest here tonight!"

That being decided, the two introduced themselves.

"I am Waldor of Kelter, and this is my wife, Joanna. We are most pleased we can help you two travelers," he said kindly.

Waldor had black hair with a great deal of gray about his temples. His full beard was a mixture of gray and black. While his face was that of an older man, Gennie and Jeff both noticed his broad shoulders and thick, strong arms. In his youth, Waldor must have been formidable. Joanna had long gray hair that was tied at the back. She was no taller than Gennie, but had a strong, commanding presence. Both her dress and Waldor's tunic were made of fine, colorful cloth.

"My name is Gennie and this is Jeff."

"Hi," Jeff said.

"Do you by any chance know what date it is?" Gennie sheepishly asked her hosts.

"The date? Why do you ask?" Joanna asked, looking cautiously to Waldor.

"Just the year," Jeff said, rubbing his leg.

"Why, it's the year of our Lord 1257," Waldor answered. "Surely you two haven't been traveling so long that you have forgotten what year it is?" he smiled.

"No," Gennie replied. "We're just very tired," which was true.

The two guests were fed a simple but filling dinner. In a tiny room attached to the cottage, Joanna made a bed for Jeff and Gennie from straw and several old blankets. It was a far cry from the comforts of home, but even Gennie admitted it felt good to rest. Just before the two nodded off to sleep, they overheard Waldor and Joanna talking in hushed voices.

"They are either orphans or runaways," Joanna said.

"That is true enough," Waldor said. "The kingdom seems to be filled with them these days. I fear the kingdom is falling into ruin."

"Philip has squandered his father's legacy and now all his subjects must pay for it," Joanna said sharply. "The man is a weakling and a fool!"

"Hold your tongue woman!" Waldor's voice rose. "No matter his many shortcomings, he is still my king, and I will not have you speak poorly of him in this house."

"I will honor your request, but my silence will not change the truth. Besides, all will be different in a few days," she said. "Do you fear these two children are spies?"

"No. Yet there is something strangely curious about them," Waldor observed.

"Yes, I sensed it as well. Something different, yet I feel I can trust them," Joanna said.

Waldor shook his gray head. "Yes, I too feel they can be trusted, though I know not what power compels me to do so."

Overhearing these words in the next room, Gennie and Jeff gave each other a quiet high-five. "Mr. Mortimer!" they said in unison. Not long after that, all in the small cottage were asleep.

CHAPTER 28

The Contest of Wisdom

The tiny, darkened room was suddenly flooded with bright sunlight.

"Awake, my sleepyheads, the day's half over!" Joanna announced, as she threw open the shutters on the windows.

The windows contained no glass, and were open to the outside air.

"You two must have traveled far yesterday to have slept so late. Waldor has gone to complete some errands in preparation for tomorrow. Are you fit enough to walk?" she asked Jeff.

"Yes, I think so," Jeff answered. His leg did feel much better this morning.

"After you eat, you two can fetch me some

water from the river," Joanna told them.

Jeff and Gennie, feeling rested and excited, scrambled from their makeshift beds, eager to help their hosts. With a large, rough bucket from Joanna, they trundled off toward the cool, clear river that churned not far from the cottage.

It seems many people in the village had come to the river for water, and the children stood back a ways, each holding the bucket's rope handles, to figure out where along the riverbank it would be easiest to get the water. An old woman with wiry gray hair came up beside them, carrying a smaller bucket and a large bundle of sticks on her back.

"Don't be shy, you two!" she barked, startling Gennie and Jeff. "Follow me!"

Without a word, they fell in behind the old woman who elbowed her way to the riverbank, then handed her bucket to the children. With both buckets filled, the two scrambled back up to join the strange woman sitting on a rock. She seemed amused at their efforts to get both buckets away from the river without sloshing too much on themselves.

"There. Job done! Now sit a spell. I saw you leaving Waldor's cottage. Are you here because of the silver coins?" she asked.

"Silver coins?" Jeff and Gennie asked.

The old woman smiled a toothless grin. "Surely you've heard the legend of the silver crowns?" she said. "Why it's known throughout the land, throughout the entire kingdom!"

Gennie and Jeff exchanged blank looks again. "No, we haven't," Jeff answered, a bit sheepishly.

"What kind of story is it?" Gennie inquired.

"Story! It's not a story but the truth!" the woman said indignantly. "I don't spin tales of fancy. This is the God's own truth. And you living under the roof of Sir Edmund's heirs. Do you take me for a fool?"

"No, no. We haven't heard the legend. Really!" Gennie tried to explain their situation to the old woman without giving her cause for alarm. "We're not from this kingdom. We're just visiting. We actually barely know Waldor. He helped when my brother Jeff got hurt and is just sort of taking care of us for a few days."

"Alright then, but it's a pity about Waldor. A fine man. A fine man indeed. But he's squandered his chances, and now Duncan's unholy brood will acquire the shire."

"What do you mean?" Jeff asked. "Waldor isn't in trouble, is he?"

"Ah, I've gotten ahead of myself. But that is better than getting behind oneself, is it not?" The old woman cackled merrily at her own cleverness. "Quiet now! I will tell you the legend. Mind you— it's true indeed. And in one day hence, the entire kingdom will discover who shall rule this shire."

"Fifty years ago, when I was but a young girl, all the kingdoms throughout the land were caught in the great holy war—the Holy Crusades against the anti-Christ from the Far East. It was a terrible time. Many sons went off to battle for many years at a time. The lucky ones returned with wounds and scars. The unlucky never returned.

"Our kingdom sent many of its finest knights to do battle. But the finest and strongest were three: Sir Mordan, Sir Roland, and Sir Edmund. Those who saw them fight said never were there three stronger, swifter, or braver men in all the land. And true enough, upon their return after years in the Holy Land, it was told they all fought with great courage and turned the tide in many a battle.

"Now, at the time, it was the custom to reward the most

courageous knights with a shire over which to rule."

"A shire?" Gennie interrupted. "What's a shire?"

The old woman looked at Gennie as if she had sprouted an extra head.

"Are you daft? A shire is a village and the nearby farms. The lord of the shire collects taxes, and all the peasants upon the land must give their lord a portion of their crops. Any man who gains a shire becomes wealthy and a favorite of the king."

"Thank you," Gennie replied.

"Now the story goes that all three knights wanted the richest shire for themselves. But King Philip liked them all equally, and did not favor one over another. So he devised a test."

"What kind of test?" Gennie asked eagerly.

"Patience, girl!" the old woman scolded.

"Have you no respect for your elders?" she snapped. "You will listen and no more. I shall tell the story as I choose to tell it. Now where was I?"

"You were telling us about a test," Jeff reminded her.

"Ah yes, the test. Now here is where King Philip showed great wisdom. Most other kings would have the three compete in some test of strength or combat. Philip said he would never doubt their courage or loyalty, but to oversee the land and the many families living upon the land, it took wisdom and shrewdness, not a strong arm and a strong sword. This was particularly true for the largest shire in the kingdom.

"So fifty years ago, he gave each knight a clay jar filled with silver crowns—a small fortune to the likes of you or me. Good King Philip said that fifty years hence, their heirs will return to this very throne. He who has the most silver crowns remaining shall be granted the richest shire in the kingdom.

"Tomorrow, it will be fifty years to the day that each of the knights received their silver. It is now the descendants of all those I spoke of who shall finish the test. Good King Philip's son, Philip the II, will carry out his father's wishes, although quite reluctantly, we hear. And the three brave knights, their bones are but dust lo these many years.

"Sir Mordan's son, Duncan, and his unpleasant wife, Shrillmora, have taken on the airs of a lord, reminding us daily that come tomorrow, we will be bowing to them. Sir Roland's son, Reginald, and Sir Edmund's son, Waldor, will not comment upon the coming proceedings. But both Reginald and Waldor have a horse and wagon, and wear fine clothing. It is all too clear that the fools have spent a portion of their father's silver crowns. For the sake of fancy garments, they will let the shire fall into the hands of Duncan and Shrillmora! A pity, too, for both Reginald and Waldor are as good as their brave fathers.

"These old bones shudder to think of the heavy toll that Shrillmora will demand from us to satisfy herself. It will be a bleak day in the shire if we must pay our taxes to the likes of them. Duncan is not half the man his father, Sir Mordan, was.

"All the kingdom will gather in the castle square tomorrow, and each descendant and their families will step forward and reveal how many silver crowns they have left."

The woman gathered together her huge bundle of firewood back onto her back, lifted her pail of water, and trudged back toward her dwelling. Gennie and Jeff were left on the riverbank, surrounded by other women and their families.

"Hi. I'm Joseph!" said a small boy who had been sitting nearby. His hair was matted and his face smeared with dirt. "I'm eight."

"Hi, my name's Jeff, and this is my sister, Gennie," Jeff said.

"I'm eleven and she's thirteen."

"You're the boy staying with Waldor, aren't you? The one who hurt his leg?" Joseph said, although he already knew the answer.

"Yes," Jeff said, rubbing his bandage.

"Do you believe the story that old woman told you?" he asked, looking around to see if anyone could overhear.

"I guess so," Gennie answered, "I'm not sure. I did hear some other people talk about some big contest tomorrow."

"Well, that's what they're talking about, and I know who's going to win!" Joseph said with great bravado.

"You do?" Jeff said excitedly. "Who?"

Joseph scooted closer to Gennie and Jeff. Once more, he looked around to make sure they were not within earshot of anyone else. In a whisper, he said, "Duncan and Shrillmora! They're rich! They still have the same jug of silver the king gave them. I know because I've seen it!"

"You've seen it?" Gennie asked.

"Yes. They get it out and look at it every night. I feel sorry for your master, Waldor. He let's me ride in his wagon sometimes. Nobody likes Duncan and his wife."

"How did you see it?" Jeff asked.

"I can't tell. But I'll show you," Joseph said encouragingly.

"You will?" Gennie exclaimed.

"I have to go now," Joseph said, standing up. "But if you want to see Duncan's treasure, you have to meet me where the road forks, when the moon is just above the castle. I'll show you then, unless you're afraid of the dark."

"We'll be there," Jeff promised. "See you tonight, Joseph!"

"Bye, Jeff," he said, running off.

"This is probably the clue Mr. Mortimer has for us," Gennie

thought aloud. "Duncan's family must have something to do with the Third Pillar of Wealth."

"We'll find out tonight," Jeff said to his sister, as they started back to Waldor's house.

CHAPTER 29

Shrillmora's Silver Coins

The moon wasn't quite over the castle when Gennie and Jeff silently slipped out of the window of Waldor's cottage. The night was fairly dark, as the moon was little more than a thin crescent. When they arrived at the fork in the road, no one was waiting for them. The only sounds they could hear were frogs and crickets.

"Great, he's not here!" Gennie said, shivering in the night air. "I can't believe we trusted him."

"Gennie, we just got here. It's not like he's wearing a watch. Let's just wait. If the legend is for real, then he'll take us right to the Third Pillar."

"What pillar?" Joseph said, as he popped up from behind a large rock. "You didn't think I'd be here did you? Well, here I am. Are you ready?"

"Let's go," Gennie said. "I'm freezing!"

The three dark figures followed the road about two hundred yards, then walked a quarter mile or so through a field. On the edge of the field, just visible in the pale moonlight, was a small, wooden cottage with a thatched roof.

"That's Duncan's house," Joseph said in a whisper. "From here on, you can't make any noises. Especially talking."

The house was dimly lit from the inside. The windows were closed and tightly shuttered. A thin trail of smoke rose lazily from the small chimney. It appeared everyone inside was fast asleep. Joseph led them around the house to the back. The rear of the small cottage was flush up against a large thicket of blackberry brambles. The huge tangle of thorns was ten feet high and extended all the way across what used to be a field. It looked to be an impossible barrier to getting any closer to the house.

"Now what?" Gennie asked. "We can't get through that. We'll get all scratched up."

"Shhh!" Joseph said. "Be quiet or we'll get caught! They're all awake inside."

Joseph led them to a spot near the massive thicket about sixty feet from the house. To Gennie's and Jeff's surprise, there was a small opening, which looked more like a rabbit hole, free from the tangle of the thorn-covered vines. Joseph crouched down and disappeared into the opening. A moment later, his head popped back out.

"Come on. It's a trail that goes under the stickers all the way to the house."

And with that, he disappeared once more. Jeff followed and disappeared into the tunnel.

"Gennie, it's like a secret passageway in here. It goes under the bushes," he called to his sister in a loud whisper. Reluctantly, Gennie got down on her hands and knees and crouched into the narrow opening.

Jeff was right. Along the ground, a natural tunnel wound its way under the mass of thorns and brambles overhead. The three had to crawl, nearly on their bellies, to slither through the brush. After several minutes, they found themselves at the back wall of Duncan's cottage.

To their left and right, and even above them, hundreds of blackberry bushes blotted out the sliver of moonlight. If not for the small tunnel-like trail that Joseph had led them to, no man, child, or beast could have penetrated the large thicket.

"Every night they take out their money and look at it," Joseph said in the quietest of whispers. "They don't even count it; they just stare at it."

Joseph silently felt about the wall until he found the loose horizontal board he knew so well. He pushed on it and it slid down, just a tiny bit, perhaps an eighth of an inch. As it moved down, it exposed a long, thin crack of yellow candlelight. Joseph put his eyes up to the crack, as did Gennie and Jeff. To the amazement of the two newcomers, they now had an unobstructed view of the interior of the one-room cottage.

Duncan of Wellstow was speaking to his wife, Shrillmora. Their three oafish teenage sons sat around the small fire, chewing on the bones leftover from the evening's supper. Only one dim, flickering candle lit the room.

Duncan spoke in a hushed tone to his sons. "You three lazy

dogs stand by the windows. We've but one day left, and we'll soon get our due."

The three lumbering young men rose and positioned themselves in front of the windows, which were all tightly shuttered. Duncan double-checked the locks on the door, then looked to Shrillmora.

"All clear," he said.

Shrillmora and Duncan went to the fire pit and, with a large iron spike, levered up one of the heavy flat hearthstones. Shrillmora reached her bony hands under the raised stone and withdrew a heavy bundle wrapped in old rags. She carefully set the bundle on the one small table in the room. Carefully, methodically, Shrillmora and Duncan unwrapped the bundle. The sons, tightly grasping their wooden staffs, looked on like hungry animals. Finally, the last of the rotten cloth fell aside and revealed a large clay jar or jug, perhaps eighteen inches high and a foot in diameter.

"They never open it," Joseph silently whispered.

The effect of the exposed jar upon the household was remarkable. The oafish sons were in awe. Duncan looked as if a great weight had been removed from his shoulders. He was relieved that tonight, like every other night for years and years, the jar was still in its resting place waiting for tomorrow's outcome. But Shrillmora fell to her knees in front of the jar. She tenderly reached out her fingers and lightly caressed the earthen container.

Gennie, Joseph, and Jeff had only seen a look like that on the faces of pilgrims kneeling at the church altar. It was unsettling.

"I've been waiting my whole life for tomorrow," Shrillmora said. "All the years of living in filth, having to grovel to merchants, and rubbing shoulders with peasants! All that will change. All that is almost over!"

"She has a screw loose," Gennie whispered.

"Yes. Let's get out of here," Jeff added. "We believe you, Joseph."

"I told you so," he said proudly.

As they started to make a silent retreat back the way they came, Gennie put her right hand down and smashed a large, fat slug.

"Yuck!" she said loudly.

"What was that?" Shrillmora asked, her rat-like eyes darting madly around the cottage. Duncan and his sons froze, listening intently.

"It was something outside," said the son closest to the back of the room.

Duncan and Shrillmora quickly wrapped the large clay jar back up in the rags and placed it under the hearthstone. At the same time, two of the sons went outside, staffs in hand, ready for a fight.

"Nice move, Gennie!" Jeff said in a barely audible whisper.

"Quiet!" she answered him.

Joseph simply lay still in the darkness. Gennie and Jeff followed his lead and lay absolutely quiet in the tunnel-like trail.

The two teenage boys walked around the perimeter of the cottage, looking hard into the darkness for any sign of an intruder. They stopped short at the thicket. They halfheartedly poked their staffs into the brush. After a minute or two of blindly poking their staffs into the thorny vines, they stopped, walked back around the house, and returned to the inside.

The three night visitors silently crawled through the thicket and back out of the opening. They were now far out of earshot of the cabin.

"That's why I don't usually bring girls along," Joseph said to Gennie.

"I've got slug guts all over my hand," Gennie said, repeatedly wiping her hand on her clothes.

"You were right about the treasure," Jeff said to Joseph. "The story's true, and they must have all the silver the king gave them."

"And that witch will have the shire," Joseph added.

"We need to get back to Waldor's house," Gennie told her brother.

"Are you going to the contest tomorrow?" Joseph asked Jeff.

"Yes, I think so. We have to!" Jeff answered, thinking of Mr. Mortimer and the Third Pillar.

Gennie and Jeff walked back through the field, onto the road, and found their way back to Waldor's house. They crept back in the window they'd left unshuttered, and slipped into their straw beds.

"Gennie, that family must be the Third Pillar," Jeff whispered.

"I guess so, but it doesn't seem to be any different from the Second Pillar," she whispered back. "They haven't spent anything for years and years. That's the same as saving, which was the Second Pillar."

"I suppose so. It's too bad they'll win the shire. They're sure a creepy bunch."

"No kidding," she answered. "Good night."

CHAPTER 30

Treasure in the Woods

A beautiful morning greeted Waldor's expanded household. Already, only an hour after dawn, the road in front of the house had many travelers upon it. Visitors from throughout the kingdom had come to see the conclusion of the great contest, and learn for themselves who would receive the richest shire in the land from King Philip.

Waldor, Joanna, Gennie, and Jeff sat around a wooden table in front of the fireplace in the small cottage. Although the dwelling was no larger than that of Duncan upon which they'd spied last night, it was many times cleaner and

179

filled with more creature comforts. The four ate coarse brown bread, boiled potatoes, turnips, and cold, leftover lamb stew.

Gennie casually picked at the food, while Jeff hungrily ate everything set in front of him.

"I'm glad to see you have a hearty appetite," Joanna said. "You'll need a full stomach to mend that leg of yours."

"How's your leg feeling today?" Waldor asked.

"It's okay, much better," Jeff said, reaching for his wooden cup of milk.

"Okay?" Waldor repeated. "You two do speak strangely."

"I got up early so I could get you a special treat!" Joanna said. "Nice, fresh goat's milk!"

She said the words "goat's milk" just as Jeff swallowed a large gulp of the warm, lumpy liquid.

"Goat's milk?" he said, with the glass still at his mouth.

"There's nothing better in the land for what ails you than fresh goat's milk."

"Fresh as in not pasteurized?" asked Gennie.

"What's pasteurized?" Joanna asked.

"Never mind," Jeff replied, setting down the glass. "It's really good; I'm just not very thirsty this morning."

Waldor pushed his plate aside and appeared quite serious.

"I have an important task for you two today. Joanna and I have discussed it, and we believe you can be trusted." Waldor put his hand onto Joanna's. "We need you to accompany Joanna to a place at the edge of the shire. I'd like you to help Joanna retrieve a certain clay jar."

"You have it!" Jeff blurted out.

"You seem particularly well-informed this morning," Waldor said, surprised by Jeff's outburst.

"Yesterday, by the river, a woman told us about the contest. How your fathers were all knights, and received a jug of silver from the king!" Gennie explained excitedly.

"And what do my young friends think of such things?" Waldor inquired.

"We hope you win!" Jeff said.

Both Waldor and Joanna laughed hard at Jeff's sentiments.

"Well, my lad," Joanna said, patting Jeff's shoulder, "we hope we do, too."

"Enough," Waldor said. "We all have much to do this morning before the tallying of silver at noon. Young Gennie and Jeff, go with Joanna to the wooded glen at the south end of Worstecher shire. There you can help her retrieve the jar of coins. I am counting a great deal on you. Please do not fail me."

"We won't," the two answered together.

"Joanna has the map. Your job will be to dig up the coins, and be watchful for highwaymen. Now be off with you!"

The three made slow progress, walking against a steady tide of pilgrims traveling toward the castle to behold the day's great event. At several places, the road become so clogged with travelers that Joanna, Gennie, and Jeff were forced to walk in the wet mud on the side of the road. However, on the outskirts of the shire, they left the main road and headed down a deserted side road. It was then the three realized a solitary traveler was following them.

The stranger maintained the same pace as the trio, staying a constant thirty feet behind. Glancing back over his shoulder, Jeff could see he was a large, disreputable looking man, who smiled menacingly when he caught Jeff's eye.

"I think that guy is definitely following us," Jeff told Gennie and Joanna.

"Oh my," Joanna said in alarm. "This is what Waldor feared!"

"Should we try to run?" Gennie proposed.

"I'm too old to outrun him," Joanna admitted. "But let's quicken our pace and see what this stranger does."

The three walked more quickly now, but the man behind them maintained the same distance. When the three slowed, hoping he would pass them by, he did the same, keeping the same space between them. They were becoming genuinely concerned.

"We're getting closer to where the jar is hidden," Joanna confided to Jeff and Gennie. "If we can just meet some travelers along the way, we could ask for help!"

They had good reason for concern. Although Jeff carried a wooden shovel, the three would be no match for the man if he carried a knife or sword.

Around a turn in the road, Joanna got her wish. A tinker and his family were approaching.

"Can you help us?" Joanna asked the man.

"In what manner might I help you?" the man inquired. He had a head and beard of fiery red hair.

"That man..." Joanna's voice trailed off as she looked behind her to where the man had been. He was gone.

"There was a man following us," she said, surprised that he was no where to be seen.

"If that is true, I imagine he's ducked into the woods. You and your children hurry along," the large man said. "I'll wait here until you're safely on your way."

"Thank you. We will take your kind offer," Joanna said. The three trotted off as fast as Joanna could run, until their red-headed guardian was out of sight. They had gone another quarter of a mile, and the stranger who had been following them was still nowhere in sight.

"This is the large oak tree Waldor told me about," Joanna said in a hushed tone. "There should be a trail into the woods just before it."

They found an overgrown trail and quickly left the road. As they made their way down the path, they were careful not to speak or make any loud noises, for fear of the stranger.

"How will we get back to the castle?" Gennie asked. "That man will be there waiting for us."

"He may wait a lifetime. That road circles back around to the shire. It will take us a bit longer to return home, but our way will be safe," Joanna said reassuringly. "Waldor's map says it lies buried beneath a rock shaped like a squatting toad. It should only be a short way off."

"There it is!" Jeff said pointing out a granite rock, which, with some imagination, did bear some resemblance to a huge frog. They stood in a small clearing, not far off the side road. They were surrounded by high bushes.

"It is here you need to dig," Joanna pointed. "Be careful when you hit something solid. We must keep the clay pot intact."

Jeff and Gennie took turns digging carefully. The work was much harder and slower than any digging they had done in the past. The ground was hard, and the wood shovel was dull. However, after five minutes of digging, a little more than a foot beneath the surface, Jeff struck a solid object.

"I found it!" he said excitedly.

"Let me see," Joanna said, getting down on her hands and knees. She wiped away some of the soil from the smooth surface Jeff had uncovered. "This is it, all right. You did well not to break it. We'd better use our hands to uncover the rest of it."

The three of them dug into the hard soil with what little finger-nails they had, hurrying as much as possible, ever mindful of the time left until they had to be at the castle. At last, enough of the dirt had been removed so Joanna could lift the pot free from the ground. She carefully wrapped it in a shawl she had brought along.

"At last," she sighed. "Now to return home."

Suddenly the stranger who had been following them earlier jumped out from behind the bushes. He knocked Jeff down, then seized Joanna by her cloak and put his greasy, pockmarked face to within inches of hers.

"Miss me, my lady?" he laughed, pushing her down. She fell hard.

Jeff reached for the wooden shovel to fight off the attacker, but two more men jumped from the bushes. A tall, stork-like looking man stamped his foot upon the shovel handle before Jeff could lift it.

"Now, what were you planning to do with that, boy?" he said menacingly at Jeff.

"We're not afraid of you!" Jeff said, as bravely as he could.

"Really?" the tall man grinned. His twisted smile revealed a jumble of teeth, brown-black from rot and decay. Unexpectedly, he struck Jeff on the side of the head with a wooden club. Jeff fell to the ground holding his ear.

"Well, you should be afraid of us, boy!" he sneered. "All of you should be!"

He looked hard at Gennie. She backed a few feet away from the men before being stopped by the underbrush that grew all around them.

"The old one has the silver," the stranger from the road said, pointing to the bundle that Joanna still clutched.

"Then I suggest 'my lady' release it to us, while we still have our good manners." The three highwaymen laughed.

The third man reached down and took the clay jar of silver from Joanna.

"Well, well, well," he said. "Perhaps the three of us will win the shire," and once again, all three laughed at their own cleverness. Jeff began to stand, and the tall, stork-like man kicked him hard on his bandaged leg. Jeff grasped his leg in pain.

"Lay still, boy!" he barked.

"You have our silver. You've no reason to hurt the children," Joanna said, rising to her feet. "Be off with you!"

This infuriated the third man, but before he could decide how to retaliate, they heard a large wagon and horses being pulled to a stop upon the road. Leery of the sound, the stranger who had followed them decided it was best to leave.

"We've got the silver, now let's be gone. There's nothing more for us here!" he said, disappearing into the brush with the jar.

"He's right, Len, we've got the money. Let's go before we have trouble," the second man said.

"I don't take kindly to this wrinkled maiden raising her voice to me," the man called Len said, tightly clutching his club, preparing to strike.

Waldor burst into the clearing. In one lightning swift action, he rapped the end of his long staff square against the forehead of the threatening highwayman. The club fell from the thug's hand as he dropped to the ground like a stone. The stork-like man named Len, who had cruelly beaten Jeff, reached into his shirt and withdrew a long knife. He scrambled to his feet and waved the knife about menacingly at Waldor.

"I am not frightened by your wooden stick, old man!" he growled

◎ Chapter Thirty ◎

through clenched teeth.

Gennie and Jeff feared for Waldor's life, for the thief was much taller, and considerably younger. Yet Waldor did not appear frightened, only determined. Waldor tossed his wooden staff aside into the brush.

"So be it!" Waldor said in a cold voice. He pulled back his cloak to reveal a sword at his waist. He smoothly withdrew the weapon from its scabbard. It was not a rusty battered sword, such as a merchant or farmer might possess, but the razor-sharp, glimmering steel sword of a knight. Neither of the highwaymen wanted any part of this. Here was not a defenseless traveler, but an armed man poised for a fight. They ran off into the dense woods as fast as they could.

"Cowards!" Waldor shouted. He sheathed the finely crafted weapon and turned his attention to Joanna.

"Are you all right? Did they harm you?" he asked.

"Only a few bruises. I will be fine. But young Jeff took the worst of their bullying."

Jeff stood up, still a bit wobbly. "He hit me in the head and kicked my leg."

Waldor examined the side of Jeff's head. "You've got a lump the size of an egg. How's your leg?"

"It hurts!" Jeff said. His bandage revealed a fresh crimson stain.

"I see. Well it could have been worse, much worse," he said. "And young Gennie, did they harm you?"

"No, I'm fine," she said thankfully.

Joanna went to her husband's side. "Waldor, the first one ran off with the jar of coins!"

"What? We'll see about that!" Waldor exclaimed. He started in the direction the thieves had run, but Joanna pulled him back by his arm.

186

"There isn't time. You must be at the castle soon," she reminded him.

"But if he doesn't get the money back it won't matter," Gennie urged.

Waldor was clearly divided upon what course of action to take. "Those black-hearted wretches should pay for this!" he said.

"It is only a jar of silver coins, my husband. One jar of silver, and the contest will begin soon. What would you have us do?" Joanna looked directly into his eyes.

"But you'll lose the silver!" Gennie blurted out. "There must be time to find them. We can help!"

"No. Joanna is right about this. There isn't time," he said, looking up at the sun's position in the sky.

"But at least you can get your money back," Gennie pleaded.

"No!" Waldor answered loudly. "I promised my father I would be at the Castle Square this day. I am bound to that. It is but *one* jar of silver. The important thing is that no one here was seriously injured. Now let us go. We must return."

It was easily apparent that Waldor was greatly frustrated that the lack of time did not permit him to hunt down the thieves for punishment.

Waldor led Joanna, Gennie, and a slightly limping Jeff back to the road where their large wagon waited. Joanna helped Jeff into the back of the wagon.

"I didn't know he had a sword," Jeff said quietly to Joanna.

"You forget the legend so soon?" Joanna asked. "Remember that Waldor is the son of Sir Edmund, who was a great knight. Sir Edmund passed his sword and armor to Waldor, and also taught him how to use them. If not for the contest at the castle, those three would have paid a dear price for striking you."

◈ Chapter Thirty ◈

Joanna and Waldor sat upon the front seat. Joanna placed a comforting hand upon Waldor's knee as he picked up the reins and urged the horses to go. Gennie and Jeff sat in the back of the large, flat wagon.

"Are you all right?" Gennie finally asked Jeff.

"No, I'm not all right," Jeff said. "My leg's throbbing and my head's killing me. Look at this bump. I can't even hear very well out my ear."

Gennie looked to be on the verge of tears.

"You don't have to cry about me, Gennie!" Jeff told her.

"It's not about you! Don't you get it?" she said. "They stole the money, Jeff! That was his money to win the shire. Now it's gone and it's our fault! We let them steal it!"

Jeff began to look despondent. He saw past his own pain to the troubles that now faced Waldor and Joanna.

"That was his father's money, Jeff." Gennie said. "What are they going to do now?"

Waldor reined back the horses to a stop. He turned around to face Jeff and Gennie.

"This is not your fault, either of you," he firmly said. "The fault is clearly mine. I should not have sent you three here unarmed to retrieve the coins. But I was finishing a matter of business." He briefly glanced at Joanna. "Let us speak no more of this. I am glad you two are safe. I would have felt far worse if one of you had been killed because of this matter.

"I will drop the three of you off at our cottage. I must conduct one more errand before the contest. I will meet you in the Castle Square."

He snapped the reins, and the wagon lurched forward, toward the castle.

CHAPTER 31

The Final Counting

The Castle Square was crowded with on-lookers who had come from throughout the kingdom to see who would win the largest and richest shire in the land. In the center of the courtyard was a small fountain where the royal court would soon be gathered. Three high-backed wooden chairs had been set atop a thick, maroon carpet. There was a throne-like chair for King Philip II, a chair for his wife, and one for the royal treasurer. It was the royal treasurer who kept the king's gold and detailed records of the taxes throughout the kingdom. The king's soldiers stood guard throughout the courtyard, and high upon the castle walls, so as to discourage bandits or highwaymen from trying to steal the silver.

Duncan and Shrillmora's clan was the first family to make their way through the tall castle gates and into the square. Duncan cradled a large bundle in his arms. Shrillmora proudly strutted through the crowd, feeling far superior to all those around her, already playing the part of nobility. Their three sons plodded behind, carrying large staffs. Their suspicious eyes darted from one onlooker to the next. They were sure that at any moment, someone would rush forward and attempt to steal their family's fortune. The family reached the fountain in the square's center and respectfully bowed to the treasurer.

"We have come to claim the Worstecher shire in the name of my father, Sir Mordran," Duncan announced to the gathering.

"Yes, yes," the treasurer said. "You are early. Each family may produce their silver when the sun is at its highest. Since you have arrived first, you will be permitted to show your silver first, once the king arrives."

Duncan's family moved to one side of the square and waited for the other families to arrive. The three sons never stopped searching the crowd, suspecting everyone to be a potential thief of their treasure.

Moments later, Reginald's family rode through the castle gates in their small cart, pulled by a tired, old horse. In the back of the cart was a bundle covered with a black blanket. They stopped the wagon in front of the fountain and climbed out, leading the cart and horse aside.

"Reginald of Lancaster, son of Sir Roland, is here for the final tally of Worstecher shire, by order of good King Philip I, fifty years ago," Reginald proclaimed to all those assembled.

At the far end of the square, the crowd began to stir. The captain

of the guards shouted out, "Make way for the king!" The crowd
parted, and hundreds of people in the square all bowed as the king
made his way through the crowd. The king's expression was one of
boredom at the entire proceedings. He took his place on the wooden
throne and waived his bejeweled hand, indicating all could rise and
cease their bowing. He addressed the treasurer.

"Are we ready to begin?"

"There is one family that has still not arrived, Your Majesty,"
the treasurer said, consulting a list of names. "It is Waldor, descendant of Sir Edmund."

"Very well," Philip said, angered at the delay. "We will wait but
a few minutes more. Why my father concocted this foolishness is
beyond reason," he said to the treasurer.

"Ah, but Sire," the crafty treasurer quietly said to the king, "if
the three have any silver crowns remaining, certainly we could ar-
range a special tax to relieve them of their coins after today's proceedings. Your own coffers are somewhat, umm, lean."

King Philip and the treasurer exchanged wicked smiles.

"You are a clever devil, are you not?" Philip said. "Yet I fear our
third descendant may not have appeared because his silver crowns
have long since been spent."

"Quite possible, Sire," the treasurer agreed.

"Yes, a pity the richest shire may go to the likes of either of these
two," the king said, looking upon Duncan and Reginald.

"Alas, you promised the Church you would uphold your father's
laws," the treasurer reminded Philip. It was a promise he'd made
years earlier.

"Yes, yes, but again a pity. Well, let's begin. I do not intend to sit out
all day amongst this rabble, waiting for a commoner." King Philip rose
to his feet and shouted, "Let us conclude my father's test!"

The crowd roared its approval that the contest was finally under way.

Waldor cracked his whip above the heads of the two horses, urging them to go faster. His large wagon nearly flew over the winding road that would eventually lead to the castle. "Faster!" he called to the two animals. "Get us to the square, and you shall never have to pull me again!"

He cracked the whip again above their heads.

"Fly, you devils. Upon my father's honor, win or lose, I will be at the Castle Square this day!" The wagon rounded a turn in the road, and there in the distance, perhaps half a mile away, towered the castle of King Philip II.

The treasurer stepped forward, unrolled a scroll, and proclaimed, "By the grace of King Philip II, and in accordance to the wishes of King Philip I, on this day it shall be decided who shall receive the shire of Worstecher!"

The crowd cheered loudly.

"Duncan of Wellstow, heir to Sir Mordran, are you present?"

"I am, Sire." Duncan bowed deeply in reverence to the king.

"Reginald of Lancaster, heir to Sir Roland, are you present?" the treasurer called out above the crowd.

"I, too, am present, Your Grace." He, too, bowed to King Philip.

"Waldor of Kelter, heir of Sir Edmund, are you present?" the treasurer called.

There was no response. The crowd looked about, murmuring their surprise. The treasurer called out again, shouting his loudest. "Waldor of Kelter, heir to Sir Edmund, are you present?"

But again, the treasurer's calls were met by silence.

"Where is he?" Joanna said. She nervously looked toward the castle's entrance. "After all these years will he be forced to break the oath he made to his father?"

"It doesn't matter anymore," Jeff said.

"It matters a great deal," Joanna corrected him.

"The fool has given up!" Shrillmora shrieked gleefully to her three sons. "He was too cowardly to show himself. The shire is as good as ours!" She hungrily rubbed her bony hands together.

The treasurer was unsure of how to proceed with one of the participants missing. The knights had been great heroes in their time. To ignore one of their descendants had never been done. "Sire?"

"Proceed," Philip said with a waive of his hand. "I grow weary of this. We will tally the other two's silver. If Waldor does not appear, then we certainly know he has long since spent his money, years ago."

"Duncan," the treasurer announced, "you shall show your silver first."

Duncan humbly approached the king and once more bowed deeply. He laid his precious bundle down upon the thick maroon carpet before the king. Slowly and methodically, he unwrapped the rags that concealed the clay jar given to his father fifty years earlier.

"Sire," Duncan began, "my father's family, and my family, have lived a frugal life. The shire of Worstecher is a great responsibility that we take most seriously. As testament to our determination, I lay before you every silver crown given to us fifty years ago by your father, King Philip I!"

And with that Duncan opened the clay jar. The jar's contents spilled upon the carpet. Hundreds of bright silver coins poured forth. The crowd surged forward to see the bountiful wealth. Even the king and treasurer were impressed that every single coin had been laid before them.

"You have done well, Duncan of Wellstow," Philip conceded. "To have deprived yourselves of such riches, for so long, which you could so easily have had, shows a will of iron. Never would I have believed that anyone, after these many, many years, would have the full measure of what my father gave to yours. Let it be known that Duncan of Wellstow has returned with the full jar of silver!"

Duncan collected his silver back into the clay jar, and returned to his wife's side.

"We've as good as won," she squealed. "Did you hear what the king said? Did you hear it? Did you?' she badgered Duncan.

"Yes, my dear, I heard. We have sacrificed these many years, year upon year upon year. Perhaps our trial is finally over," Duncan said wearily.

Waldor's trial, unfortunately, was far from over. Waldor's wagon had been stopped several hundred yards from the castle's huge gate. It was surrounded by eight of the king's guards.

"You cannot go any farther with a wagon of this size," one of the uniformed guards said. "The castle is overflowing with people. There is no room for such a wagon. Haven't you heard? It's the day the shire of Worstecher is to be decided."

"Of course, I've heard. I'm Waldor of Kelter, son of Sir Edmund. I must reach the castle's square immediately."

"And I'm the king himself," the guard replied sarcastically.

"Please, my good man, I'm most serious. You must believe me! Upon an oath to my father, I must be in that square!"

The guard drew his sword, and several others did the same.

"Perhaps, Sir 'Jester', we will need to teach you some manners," the guard said, smiling.

The treasurer's loud voice called out above the crowd. "Reginald of Lancaster, come forward so we may tally your silver."

The crowd, much of it from the Worstecher shire, keenly leaned forward. They hoped against hopes that somehow, someway, Reginald would also have all his silver, and somehow might be awarded the shire. Every man, woman, and child in the shire loathed the thought of being lorded over by Shrillmora. Alas, Reginald's fine clothing, his cart and horse, his small farm, all indicated that at least a portion of his father's silver crowns had been spent.

Reginald led his small cart to the center of the square. As he passed Shrillmora, he gave her the most curious look, as if she was of absolutely no concern to him. It troubled her. From under the blanket in the back of the small cart, Reginald withdrew a clay jar. It was an exact duplicate of the jar Duncan had shown moments earlier. Reginald held it up before the King.

"Your Majesty, I, too, have the original jar of silver crowns your father gave to mine fifty years ago. And like Duncan of Wellstow, within this jar is every single crown it originally held!"

Reginald emptied the jar upon the carpet, and it, too, poured forth a mound of silver coins. The crowd began to laugh with relief, for it now appeared they had escaped the temper and wrath of Shrillmora.

"How can this be?" Shrillmora screamed at her husband. "He has cheated somehow! Look at his clothes! We should have won! The shire should be ours!"

"You have done well, Reginald of Lancaster," the king said. "But I am now presented with a most difficult problem. Both you and Duncan have returned with the full measure of silver crowns. You have both saved wisely and now are both entitled to the shire. I did not anticipate such an outcome."

"But my good King," Reginald said humbly. "Allow me to assist in your decision, for whereas Duncan has returned with but one jar of silver, I have returned with two!"

Reginald withdrew a second jar from his small cart, opened it, and poured another pile of silver coins in front of the king, as high as the first. The king and treasurer were stunned. The crowd cheered wildly, for now they had surely escaped Shrillmora's rule.

"How was this done?" the king asked. "Your money has multiplied! Is this some sort of trick?"

"It is no trick, Sire," Reginald said.

The king turned to his royal treasurer and asked," Is such a thing permitted, per my father's will?"

"Most certainly, Sire," the treasurer replied, once again consulting an old scroll that laid down the original rules of King Philip I's test. "Each man was free to do with his silver as each saw fit. Be that spending their wealth, or be that *investing it,*" he said narrowing his eyes knowingly at Reginald. "For that is what you have done, is it not, Reginald of Lancaster? You and your father invested the silver coins so that they would grow?"

"It is indeed, my lord," Reginald answered. "While Duncan squirreled his money away from the light of day, my father and I lent it to those in need of it, but who could repay us over time, with a small extra amount for our trouble."

"Clever," King Philip said.

"Yes, it's called 'interest,' Your Majesty," the treasurer explained. "When we had more money in the royal treasury, it was a practice we sometimes did."

"Over many years, as our money was returned, we would put the extra silver into this second jar," Reginald continued. "After many years, it filled the second jar, and allowed us enough extra to make our lives more comfortable, Sire."

"Ingenious!" said the king. "Clearly you have shown wisdom in making your money grow. Certainly, the shire of Worstecher will not be given to Duncan of Wellstow."

"Ahhhh!" A high-pitched scream filled the courtyard and pained the ears of every man and woman present. It was Shrillmora.

"No, no, no!" she cried, running to the center of the square. "All these years, year after year we lived like rats! Never spending, wearing rags, eating the refuse of others. All for this day, to be pronounced the Lady of Worstecher. It cannot be! I am the Lady of Worstecher, I am the rightful Lady of Worstecher!"

Screaming like a mad woman, she ran from the Castle Square and out the castle gate.

Duncan and his three sons were horrified. "A thousand pardons, my King. The many years of waiting for this day have taken their toll upon my wife. I request your permission to leave these festivities so that I may retrieve my wife."

"Permission granted," the king replied, his eyes wide as saucers over the woman's remarkable outburst.

Duncan and his large sons wearily walked from the castle, once again cradling the jar of silver coins.

The king rose to his feet. "Reginald of Lancaster, come forward. You have shown yourself quite shrewd. Not only have you returned with the original jar of silver coins, but you have created a second. I can see no reason not to bestow the shire of Worstecher to you this day!"

CHAPTER 32

Waldor's Miracle

From out of nowhere, six of the king's soldiers frantically rode through the castle gate at a full gallop and into the courtyard, scattering the panicked people like chickens. These were the same soldiers who moments earlier had stopped Waldor on the outskirts of the walled city.

"Your Highness!" the lieutenant called out. "Stop the contest!"

The six galloped up to the fountain and dismounted. They immediately fell to their knees in deference to their king.

"What is the meaning of this?" the king demanded sternly. "You interrupt this gathering and endanger my subjects with your recklessness.

Explain yourselves immediately and hope I am lenient with your fate."

"Your Majesty, is this not the day of judgment for the Worstecher shire?" a frightened soldier stammered, still on his knees.

"It is indeed," the treasurer answered. "Every man in the kingdom knows this. That does not excuse this outburst!"

"I have beheld a miracle, Sire!" the soldier said to the king. "I beg you to delay the awarding of the shire until..."

"Until what, you impertinent dog," the king shouted angrily. "Why should I delay? What is the miracle of which you speak? Answer me!"

"The miracle, Your Majesty," and as the lieutenant said these words he looked over to the castle gate to see Waldor furiously driving his wagon through the gates of the castle. The soldier, momentarily forgetting the presence of the king, rose to his feet and pointed toward Waldor's wagon.

"The miracle, Your Majesty, it approaches now!" the soldier said.

Careful of the crowd of onlookers, Waldor reigned back his horses to slow the large wagon as it entered the square. At the center of the square, he stopped the wagon and clambered to the ground. Bowing deeply, he said, "Forgive my entrance, Your Majesty, but I was unexpectedly delayed. I am Waldor of Kelter, son of Sir Edmund. I have come for the tallying of silver for the shire of Worstecher."

"What gives?" Jeff asked Gennie in a loud whisper. "He has no money left. We lost it!"

"He shouldn't have come," Gennie added, directing her comments to Joanna. "He'll only embarrass himself."

"Shhh," Joanna said, "watch and learn the secret we have hidden these fifty years."

The gathering of people now crowded ever closer to the center of the square. They were all quite curious why Waldor had made his dramatic entrance, for even if he possessed all his silver, how could he have more than Reginald, who had proven himself as clever as the king's own treasurer?

"This man speaks of miracles," King Philip said, gesturing to the soldier. "Let us hope for the sake of his head that you have something of importance to share with us. Do proceed."

Waldor returned to his wagon. The entire wagon bed was filled with some manner of cargo, but had been covered up with a large, dark cloth. Waldor reached under the cloth and withdrew a clay jar, similar to the jars displayed by Duncan of Wellstow and Reginald of Lancaster.

"Your Highness, in my hands I have a jar of silver crowns. The same measure of coins your father presented to mine so many years ago," Waldor said.

He poured the coins out on to the maroon carpet, just as the others had.

"But that's not possible," Gennie said. "He has no silver left! It was stolen."

"He must have captured it back from the thieves," Jeff concluded.

"I doubt it," his wife said quietly.

The king and treasurer smiled at one another.

"You have done well to save your silver, but this is far short of a miracle, of which this young lieutenant mistakenly spoke, and to which he will be punished."

Despite the king's threats, the soldiers now seemed quite confident. To the king's astonishment, the soldier was actually smiling.

Reginald approached Waldor.

"It is true, Waldor. Before you arrived, I displayed the silver my family and I have accumulated. It may shock you, but I have not one jar of silver coins, but two!" Reginald said proudly. "I have invested my silver so it would grow."

"I had suspected as much, Reginald. And I commend you for your shrewdness," Waldor said genuinely. "But you have only discovered half the secret, my honorable friend, while I was fortunate to discover the second half of the secret. And to be sure, it is the second half that is the most important part of the riddle."

"Enough banter," the king shouted. "I was told of a miracle! Has this measly jar of silver been mistaken for a miracle by this poor fool?" King Philip pointed to the soldier.

"No, your Highness," Waldor said, returning to the side of his wagon. "This is the miracle of which he spoke."

And with a grand sweep of his arm, Waldor ripped off the large cloth from atop his wagon, to reveal twenty clay jars. "For while Reginald turned one jar of silver into two, I have turned one jar of silver into twenty!"

"Impossible!" Reginald shouted.

"Do you take us for fools?' the king said.

"Soldiers, break open these jars so we may expose this man for the fraud he is," the treasurer called out.

One of the king's own special guards drew his sword and strode to the wagon. He violently smashed one of the clay jugs and a river of silver poured forth, spilling over the bed of the wagon.

"Smash them all," the treasurer screamed. "It is a trick!"

Again the guard smashed one of the large earthen containers, but it too was filled with hundreds of silver crowns. Again and again he smashed the clay jars, and each time a bounty of silver overflowed into the wagon. After he had crushed the last of the jars, and like all the others, it had yielded a wealth of coins, the man backed away from the wagon. Now the wagon truly overflowed with a mountain of silver, mixed with the broken shards of clay.

The king's guard was stupefied.

"Your Highness," he said in a hushed tone, "it truly is a miracle!"

The crowd had become still and quiet. No man, woman, or child had ever dreamed that in all their lives they would behold such a treasure. It was an incredible sight. Gennie and Jeff were as dumbstruck by the outpouring of coins as the others.

How could it have been done? What was the secret?

The treasurer was speechless. Even he had never seen so much silver at one time. King Philip broke the silence that had descended upon the square.

"Explain yourself, Waldor of Kelter. Is this the work of sorcery, or has the son of Sir Edmund become a highwayman? How did this come to pass?"

"Neither, your Highness, for my father and I, like Reginald, invested our silver so it would grow; but with one small difference. When Reginald earned interest upon his money, he hid the interest in a second jar. Over many years he concealed all his earnings in a hidden jar."

"That is true," Reginald confirmed. "How could you have earned so much more than I?"

"Because, Your Majesty, I did not hide my earnings in a jar to gather dust. I added those earnings to the money I was investing. As such, I earned interest upon my interest."

"But that would be a trifling sum," Reginald said, challenging Waldor's words. "That would not explain so vast a treasure!"

"Ah, but you are wrong! Over the years the interest grows to a huge amount. As you can see before you, it grows to an amount far greater than the original gift of silver. My father, Sir Edmund, learned of this secret in his travels to the Far East from an ancient wise man.

He called it *compounding."*

"What says my treasurer?" the king asked.

The treasurer conducted rapid calculations in his head. All eyes in the square were upon him. He mumbled to himself and wrote numbers in the air with his eyes closed. He was calculating year after year of Waldor's remarkable formula. After several long minutes had passed, the treasurer's eyes popped open with a start.

"It is true! Why in the fortieth year of such a plan the interest alone will be a full jar of silver. Just the interest for just one year! The money does indeed compound itself."

The king rose from his throne. Ever so slowly, he walked to Waldor's wagon. He reached his hands into the huge pile of silver coins. Lifting two great handfuls, he let them run through his fingers, falling back onto the pile.

"Then it is true," the king said softly. "The miracle truly does exist. What man or king would deny Waldor the shire of Worstecher now?"

The treasurer slunk to the king's side.

"Sire, would this not be a good time to inform Waldor of the special tax we have?" he hissed into Philip's ear. "It would be a shame to strain his horses under so great a load."

"I think not," the king commanded loudly. "Waldor has given us something of far greater value than this wagonload of coin. He has given us the wondrous secret by which to multiply money. We would all do well to heed his wisdom."

The king announced to all gathered in the square, "I proclaim the shire of Worstecher shall be granted this day to Waldor of Kelter, who shall forever more be known a Waldor, Lord of Worstecher."

The entire crowd, including Gennie and Jeff, roared in approval for the new Lord of Worstecher, Waldor. No one in the crowd, not even Joanna, noticed the fog-like mist gathering around Gennie's and Jeff's feet.

CHAPTER 33

Homeward Bound

"That was amazing!" Jeff said, his voice echoing throughout the huge chamber of pillars. "Waldor surprised everybody!"

"Especially us," Gennie admitted. "I thought all his money had been stolen! Nobody knew he'd been investing it."

Mr. Mortimer silently pointed an outstretched hand toward the final unnamed pillar. The children walked over to it. On its massive base were the letters I-N-V-E-S-T. They returned to where Mr. Mortimer stood. Their footsteps echoed throughout the huge hall.

"Come and walk with me," Mr. Mortimer said. "I don't have much time left with you."

The three walked slowly together around the circumference of the great hall, in and out of the shadows cast by the many flickering oil lamps.

"And upon this journey, what did you learn?" the ancient man asked.

"Well, Duncan didn't win the shire because he never did anything with his money, didn't invest it, I mean," Jeff said.

"And Waldor won because he was able to multiply his money by investing it," Gennie added.

"Good. Well observed," the old man grinned. "As you now have learned, the industrious person desiring wealth works hard and carefully saves. But the wisest of all not only saves money, but also puts it to work. That is what investing does—your money works for you.

"While Duncan and his family saved every silver crown their ancestor had received, they hid their money away like some terrible secret," Mortimer continued. "And like a plant shut away from the light, their money could never grow.

"Waldor, on the other hand, had the wisdom to let his money work for him. He invested it *and* he continued to let it grow. As such, in time it grew to become a great deal of money. To attain wealth, it is not enough to simply hold onto money, you also must grow the money you save.

"You now have truly learned the Three Pillars of Wealth," Mr. Mortimer said. "You understand that wealth all begins with a burning desire to achieve it. That all else grows from this desire. You learned that wealth cannot be attained without saving—postponing gratification from the present to the future. And you learned the importance of compounding and investing your money. To attain wealth one must do more than simply hide it away."

Gennie and Jeff nodded in agreement. They truly did understand the Three Pillars, and the ways to attain wealth.

"Then you can learn no more from me," Mr. Mortimer said sadly. "My work here is done."

"But won't we ever see you again?" Gennie asked.

"Perhaps you shall think of me from time to time, but it is the lessons you have learned that are important, not I," Mr. Mortimer said.

Slowly the mist began to circle around Gennie's and Jeff's feet. Gennie jumped forward and gave the little old man a hug. Jeff, a bit embarrassed at first, did the same.

"Thank you very much," Mr. Mortimer smiled. "This is how I shall remember the both of you."

And with that, the mist swirled ever faster and higher around the two children, until Gennie and Jeff could no longer see the great Chamber of Pillars, or the ancient figure of Mr. Mortimer.

Gennie and Jeff awoke with a start, as their front door slammed shut. They had fallen asleep on their porch steps. Their parents were standing in front of the door.

"What are you two doing out here?" their father asked.

"It's the middle of the night!" their mother said.

"What time is it?" Jeff asked.

Gennie instinctively looked at her watch. "It's only 1:30," she said. "I thought it was later!"

"I had the weirdest dream," Jeff said. "It went on and on."

"Me, too. It was wild," Gennie said, still looking down at her watch in confusion.

"Is something wrong?" Mr. Douglas asked the children.

"Well, we came outside because we got tired of listening to you guys argue," Jeff said sheepishly.

"Argue?" Mr. Douglas exclaimed. "We weren't arguing. We've agreed to make a go of it."

Mr. and Mrs. Douglas reached out and took each other's hands.

"We just need to get some professional financial advice."

"Let's all go inside," Mrs. Douglas said. "It's getting cold."

Jeff winced in pain as he took a step up the porch stairs.

"Ow!" he said, rubbing his shin.

"What's the matter?" Mrs. Douglas said, stepping down to Jeff's side.

Jeff pulled up the leg of his sweatpants. Upon his shin was a large scar from a partially healed wound.

"Jeff! When did that happen?" Mrs. Douglas said with concern. "I don't remember seeing that before."

Gennie and Jeff gaped at each other in wide-eyed disbelief.

"I think it's pretty recent," Jeff quietly said.

As the family walked up the steps to the door, Gennie said, "You know, maybe Jeff and I have some ideas about money you might want to hear."

Mr. Douglas put his arm around Gennie's shoulder.

"Well, at this point, it sure wouldn't do any harm to listen," he said.

They walked into the house and the door slowly closed behind them. As the gentle breeze subsided, a faint tap-tinkle-tap-tinkle could be heard, far away in the distance.